Praise for ANDREW ~~VACHSS~~ and

THAT'S HOW I ROLL

"Vachss's stories . . . burn with righteous rage and transfer a degree of that rage to the reader."
—*The Washington Post Book World*

"Esau Till has to be about the most unique killer-for-hire ever invented. . . . A great character study of a man with a mission, despite overwhelming odds. His survival instincts and matter-of-fact philosophies promise to remain unrivaled for quite some time."
—*Bookreporter*

"Vachss's tough-guy writing style grabs you by the hair and jerks you to attention."
—*Detroit Free Press*

"This novel could easily be mistaken for a memoir. . . . Both chilling and realistic."
—*New York Journal of Books*

"Vachss combines his trademark black humor with his longstanding concern for children and their well-being. . . . A smart, cynical glimpse into the human condition."
—*Kirkus Reviews*

"[A] chilling tour de force
courtly manners, deadl~~y~~
purpose."

ALSO BY ANDREW VACHSS

THE BURKE SERIES

OTHER NOVELS

SHORT-STORY COLLECTIONS

Andrew Vachss
THAT'S HOW I ROLL

Andrew Vachss is a lawyer who represents children and youths exclusively. His many novels include the Burke series and two collections of short stories. His books have been translated into twenty languages, and his work has appeared in *Parade*, *Antaeus*, *Esquire*, *Playboy*, and *The New York Times*, among other publications. He divides his time between his native New York City and the Pacific Northwest.

www.vachss.com

THAT'S HOW I ROLL

Andrew Vachss

VINTAGE CRIME / BLACK LIZARD
Vintage Books
A Division of Random House, Inc.
New York

FIRST VINTAGE CRIME/BLACK LIZARD EDITION, JANUARY 2013

The Library of Congress has cataloged the Pantheon edition as follows:
Vachss, Andrew H.
That's how I roll / Andrew Vachss.
p. cm.
1. Assassins—Fiction.   2. Death row inmates—Fiction.   3. Political corruption—
Fiction.   4. Incest—Psychological aspects—Fiction.   I. Title.
PS3572.A33T53 2011 813'.54—dc22 2011013503

Vintage ISBN: 978-0-307-94867-0

Book design by Robert C. Olsson

www.weeklylizard.com

Printed in the United States of America
10 9 8 7 6 5 4 3 2 1

my beloved brother Olaf

29 December 2010 @ 11:30 p.m.

he chose the night to depart
bringing a new star to the sky

a warrior's star, casting its own light
a guidepost to the path of righteousness
a warning to predators
and now the True North for all our tribe

my brother:

welcomed by Odin
waiting for us
and always, always watching

THAT'S HOW I ROLL

My name is Esau Till.

What I've put down here isn't some "Death Row Diary," like the bloodsuckers wanted to pay me to write. Don't look for a last-minute confession to crimes I was never caught for. Or for the apology some think I owe.

This is a bomb. The last one I'll ever build. You'll never even know it exists unless someone stumbles over the tripwire I left behind.

That will happen only if I am betrayed. I don't expect that, but I still have to plan for it.

No bomb I made ever failed, which is why people paid me so much to build them. In my chosen line of work, you have to earn a reputation before you start earning real money.

My bombs were always custom-tailored to the job. Now, the only ingredients I have for building this last one are my own words. Those words should be more than enough, but they won't ignite unless they are believed.

I know if I'm caught in one single lie people might well disbelieve my entire account . . . and they'd be entitled to do so. All it takes is a single clutch of termite eggs to bring down a whole house.

People say the truth can't be killed. Maybe not. But from my own experience, I know it can be buried so deep it might as well never have existed at all.

Oh, you might get your ear close enough to the ground to hear it ticking. But no matter how close you listen, you're still just hearing strange noises deep down in the dark.

Your eyes won't help, either. The brighter the light you shine, the more the darkness thickens.

Only the most powerful explosive will light the way. So this bomb must be like the most carefully constructed house.

I know it must stand up to the most microscopic examination. And it must <u>stay</u> standing, no matter what attempts are made to defuse it.

For <u>this</u> house, each brick will be embedded in the cement of gospel truth. No flood will ever carry it away. No fire will ever incinerate it. And the most powerful wrecking ball would just bounce right off.

I never broke my word when I was alive. That's the one thing I get to take with me, and I intend on doing just that. I'm building this house out of nothing but truth, and no more powerful explosive has ever been invented. Once revealed, it will be denied by some, and "explained" by others.

But it can't be changed.

When that last button is pushed, the roof will fly off. Inside, just a few empty rooms.

And a map.

I'm marking that map with an "X" for each spot.

If you're looking for buried treasure, don't waste your time. But if you dig deep enough, if you <u>keep</u> digging, you will find that pure truth I promised. It's all there.

Whether that truth frees you or destroys you no longer matters to me.

I'm done.

Me and Tory-boy, neither of us came out right. I was born with this spine thing. I'm past forty years old, and I've never once stood on my own feet.

Tory came along about eight years after me. He was a big, handsome baby. It took a while before you could tell he carried the same curse I did.

I've been protecting Tory-boy all his life. I won't stop doing that just because the State is getting ready to end mine.

Nobody expects anything less from me. They have confidence that I'll come up with some way to keep right on protecting my little brother.

People who truly know me, they know I'll find a way. It took a lot of time and a lot of lives, but I finally forced that knowledge upon them—etched it too deep into their minds for them to ever believe otherwise.

If you're reading this, you'll come to know my life.

Not the fairy story I told on TV, or in court. You'll know what parts I left out of those stories.

By that, I don't mean the crimes I never spoke of, or how I got them done. What good would it do if I explained how I could make our satellite dish throw out a plasma-cutter beam? People already know enough ways to kill other people. They seem to be getting better at it. The whole human race, I mean.

So, when you come across certain people's names in here, keep in mind that I am breaking no vows. Yes, I know I'm building a graveyard. But I'm really only marking the tombstones—those who betrayed me put themselves beneath them.

I don't feel any guilt. When it comes to such things, I don't feel much of anything. And what I *do* feel is no more complicated than this: I know the difference between the best possible result and the best result possible.

The best possible result would be for everyone to keep their word. Then my Tory-boy would still be protected, even long after I'm gone.

But if certain people break their word—and you'll not be reading this if they haven't done so—all that's left is the best result possible.

Revenge.

I never trusted a word out of a government man's mouth from the time I was old enough to understand how they were to blame for everything that had happened to all of us.

If the government could look away from—well, you'll see for yourselves—they're even worse than the Beast they had kept on feeding for so long. If it wasn't for me, they'd still be doing it.

There's only two people on this earth I trust.

My little brother is one of those two, and he would never reveal who the other one is. All I had to do was say "secret" to Tory-boy, and *nothing* could ever make him tell it.

Maybe you'll think badly of me when I tell you this, but I promised the truth, so I have to say how I know Tory-boy would keep anything I told him was "secret" to himself, no matter what. He was still very small when I started training him. As soon as I thought he was ready, I hid some money—just a couple of dollars and some coins—and I told Tory-boy where I'd stashed it. Then I told him it was "secret." And then I let it slip to Rory-Anne that I'd hidden some money.

She knew better than to try and make me tell, but Tory-boy was not even four years old. And she did things to him I can't write down, not even here. Listening to my brother scream cut me so deep I don't have the words for it. And knowing it was me who had caused those screams cut me deeper . . . cut me in a place I didn't know I had. But I had to know. If Tory-Boy couldn't keep a secret . . .

He wouldn't tell. Three times, Rory-Anne tried. My brave little brother would not tell. Twice he passed out from the pain. After the second time, Rory-Anne came to me. She told me, straight out, what she was going to do to Tory-boy if he didn't tell. Or if I didn't. She wanted that money, and she was going to get it, even if she had to kill us both.

I looked her right in her degenerate eyes and said I didn't know what she was talking about.

After that third time, she gave up.

That's when I could finally hold my little brother. I begged his forgiveness. He didn't understand what I was saying, but he knew—I *know* he knew—what I meant.

Tory-boy would never tell any secret of mine.

I know things can just happen. And I know my Tory-boy. He could die in a car accident. Or get himself shot over nothing. Killed by the kind of man who'd lose a fair fight and back-shoot the winner as he walked away. Where we live, even the most diligent watchers couldn't prevent something like that.

But the only one capable of detonating my last bomb, *that* person would know the difference.

THAT'S HOW I ROLL

If you are reading this, I have been betrayed. So this is being revealed to you, just as I promised. Revealed by someone I know would never betray me.

I have someone nobody knows of; someone not in the life I chose for myself. Someone pure. Someone who could deliver my last bomb with a clear conscience. To that person, delivering my message wouldn't be informing; it would be doing the right thing.

They might decide to wait a good long while. That's because they're in this story, too—I couldn't leave them out even if I wanted to.

But somehow I don't believe it will happen like that. The person I am trusting with this wouldn't *want* me to wait; they'd want me to show the whole world as soon as possible how I kept my word.

My last word.

I know this all would be easier to understand if I started at the beginning and went from there. But the place where I was born, the place where I spent my entire life, it's got a time rhythm all its own. It's more than a dot on a map—it's a living thing, as immune to the laws of physics as it is to the laws of man. Sometimes, things don't happen in normal sequence. If you were born and raised there, you'd feel it, too. As if the earth itself stopped rotating in one direction, reversed itself, and then went back to the way it was turning before.

I don't mean to say that this is the only such place on earth. I *know* there's others. I can't say how I know this, but I can feel that truth of knowledge inside me.

So I can't tell my story any other way except how I'm writing this down. The only way for me to tell the truth is to tell it as I experienced it.

I know I'm not helping you believe me, telling my story this way. But no matter how it may sound sometimes, this is no tale of magic; it is cold, hard fact. And if you read my story, you'll know why I had no choice but to tell it.

T

his is how I saw it happening:

A mob of bears surrounded the hive, ripping at it like tall-timber chainsaws, desperate to get at the sweet stash of honey they knew was inside.

Bears chasing honey don't worry themselves about filing environmental-impact statements. They know they don't need any of those weasel-word excuses for tearing things up—nobody is ever going to call them to account. You could pass a dozen laws a day, it wouldn't make any difference to them.

Legislation is just words. The real law is the law *enforcers*. It doesn't matter what you call them—sheriffs, police officers, cops—those people, they're the only true law.

But, for all that, they're still not the ones in charge.

N

o matter how fierce the attack got, the hive stayed quiet. No swarm of drones rushed out, stinging, to protect the inner core. Layer after layer yielded to the slashing claws, but the core itself stayed untouched, as if in some impenetrable glass cage. The bears could see it, but they couldn't touch it.

It didn't matter to the bears what kind of stingers might be waiting on them. They knew honeybees weren't close to the worst they might have to face. They knew all about hornets, mahogany wasps . . . all the way down to fire ants. All nest-guarders come loaded with serious venom, and they're always willing to spend every bit they have.

But that didn't discourage the bears. For all they gave a damn, the hive could have been surrounded by five-pound scorpions. Those bears knew the value of that special core of honey, and they were ready to pay whatever it cost to get at it.

No matter what force was protecting that honey, they knew they could take the pain, walk right through it. What they didn't know was that the greatest danger to them was that honey itself.

Bees might succeed in discouraging a single bear, but they can't kill one. They have the desire, but they don't have the power.

Bears *can* kill each other, but they've got too much sense to do that. When mating season comes, if any two males catch each other's scent, there's going to be blood, sure. But that's blood, not death. Soon as one bear realizes he's not going to come out on top, he moves on.

You might think it's their place on the evolutionary chain that gives bears that much sense. Sharks are natural-born killers, but they don't have the intelligence to get out of the way when they're facing something that could turn them into a meal. Even with the best electrical sensors on the planet, they can't tell the difference between pieces of an abandoned ship slowly sinking to the ocean floor and a pod of killer whales with newborn calves.

Whatever drives sharks doesn't have a reverse gear. The instant they pick up a trace of blood in the water, they go straight to whatever's shedding that blood, and commence to ripping a chunk off for themselves.

That makes more blood. And that brings more sharks. Soon enough, they're in such a foamy red frenzy that it doesn't make any difference where the blood's coming from . . . even from themselves. Before long, they're all slashing blind. That's not a good time to be a shark.

I've never seen a real shark, and now I know I never will. But ever since I read that there's a special kind of shark that can actually go from the ocean right into a river, and back out again, that just fascinated me. A bull shark—that's what they're called—is also the only shark that has a memory. There's no place to hide from something like that, unless you spend all your life on dry land.

The more I read about that special shark, the more I wanted to be one myself. More like a mirror image of one, I guess—I wanted to become the kind of creature nobody would be safe from on dry land.

Maybe I'm just making myself sound too important—I know I have to guard against that. But I think there's some value in me writing this down. I don't have any such pretensions about the account of my life, but I know there's been times when a record of truth actually changed the world. Some of it, anyway.

Actually *changing* things, that's a high bar to clear. No conspiracy theory could ever do it. No interpretation of the Good Book, no "expert analysis." What's required is scientific truth.

I know what you're thinking just about now. You never heard of "scientific truth." No reason why you would. I made up that term because nothing else can explain what I did and why I did it.

I won't deny that some part of me wants to brag on myself. Maybe all the years I've spent in this cell caused me to finally grow an ego—or maybe just acknowledge something I had never allowed to interfere during all those years of doing my work. Any ego surfacing in me, that's only *now*. Only after I was caught.

Unlike so many others in here, I wasn't caught because of my own boasting. Nor from taking false pride in the things I was able to do. If you burn a building to the ground, you have to first make sure that you know every single person who's in that building. And make *real* sure that you're willing for them to burn, too.

I understand all kinds and types of people may be reading this.

So, whoever you are, don't mistake my motives. I don't owe you— *any* of you—one damn thing. I never asked you for anything in my life, and I'm not asking now.

Don't waste your time trying to decode me. Save your "profiles." Forget any "psychiatric autopsies." You'll never know me. What you're reading isn't some "story." It's *my* story, but it's all fact. If you actually knew me, you'd know my story couldn't be any other way.

What I'm writing down here will pay off the only debt I have left—my life story is an accountant's ledger. It will pay anything on my debit side, and I'm not asking for a discount.

That's what I want people to say about me after I'm gone: "Esau Till, that was a man who paid his debts. Every single one. And he always paid in full."

No mainframe computer could have predicted the intersection of runaway trains that caused me to get caught. And whatever put me in a position where I could get caught, *that's* a true mystery. No matter how much I think back on it, no matter how deep I go, probing with the long, sharp-tipped points of my mind, I still can't reach that part.

The mind protects itself, so I understand I might be avoiding the truth. I understand that maybe it took nothing more than a single petty emotion to bring me down. Envy is a sin. Not because the Bible says so, but because it can make you do stupid things. When you're born and raised like I was, you figure it out quick: if the only thing keeping you alive is your intelligence, acting stupid is committing suicide.

So, despite my circumstances, I never coveted what others had. And when I learned how I could change those circumstances, there was no need for me to envy such things, anyway: houses, cars, jewelry, things like that. Things, that's one key. But understanding yourself means you have to be able to open a two-key lock.

You might be able to look back and see where you went wrong. But that's a vision, not a tool. You can't use what you see in your past to go back and change it. Sure, you can buy things you never had before, but you can't change the "before."

When I found that second key, I realized envy is no sin—it can even be a motivation. Wanting what others have, that's not wrong. It can make you strive. Work harder. Reach higher.

You *can* change your own future.

You might want a Cadillac. So might another man. You each envy the man who has one. And you each have choices. You can work and save your money until you have enough for that Caddy. You can steal money other people worked for; it spends just as good as money honestly earned. Or you can just sit there, stewing in your own bile. That's poisonous stuff, bile.

When two men each want a Cadillac, they can go their separate ways to get one. Usually, they keep going those separate ways for the rest of their lives.

It's only when you and another want the same thing—not an assembly line thing, something there's only one of—that *real* sin knocks on your door. If you open the door, greed and possessiveness come right on in and make themselves to home. Once they're in, they never leave.

Two men want the same woman. This can bring blood, but that's pretty rare. Most of the time, the man who's not the woman's choice gets over being rejected.

Sometimes, the woman doesn't even know she's wanted by that man. He might believe he wouldn't be her choice, and keep his own feelings to himself. So there's no rejection to resent . . . or regret.

But what about the man who *does* get what he wanted so bad?

He could treat his woman like a princess. Be grateful every day of his life that he got so lucky. Work three jobs to buy her nice things.

Or he could treat her like a slave. Not just making her work, but beating on her when she doesn't work hard enough. Hard enough to support him when he quits his job or gets laid off.

Hard enough to make him forget he's got twice the stomach and half the hair he used to have.

Some men, the only work they do is keep watch on their woman—go through the phone bills to see if there's any strange numbers there; sit outside a tavern where she's playing a few games of eight-ball with her friends to see who she leaves with; third-degree question her every time she comes back into the house.

And some are too lazy to do even that much. They just keep their woman in the house. Cut her off from her friends, even from her own family.

That sometimes works. But it's got strong potential for back-fire, too. If a man catches his woman in bed with another man, and he ends the affair with a pistol, the jury's not going to treat him too harshly. They call it the "unwritten law."

But that only works for men. If a woman's husband staggers in one night, drunk and nasty, a whore's lipstick smeared all over him, she might be able to shoot him and get the law to treat her lightly, too. But only if she remembers to say he was acting like he was about to kill her. Self-defense. Around here, that means she only gets to fire once. A shotgun works a lot better than a pistol for that.

Now that I'm taking stock, I have to face up to things like that. Admit that it might have been something as small and petty as my own possessiveness that brought all this down.

"Might have," that's speculation. But this, this is absolute truth: I was never going to let anyone or anything take my little brother from me. That was never going to happen, no matter what the cost, or who had to pay it.

'd seen these same bears plenty of times—I'd been seeing them one way or another ever since I started earning money. The bears were all after the same thing. They all worked the same way. I'd seen them tear hives apart often enough. But this was the first time I'd ever *been* that hive-protected honey.

The kind of men I did work for, some of them would talk about how terrible the bears could make it for you if you stopped them from getting their paws on the honey. How much strength it took to hold them off. How that tested a man, deep inside.

Bragging? I don't know. Maybe the men who never said a word about such things were the only ones who had really passed that test.

But I didn't have to believe any of those stories to know how to behave when those bears came for me. All I had to do was act the way the storytellers claimed they had.

The whole thing was kind of stupid, because the one thing the bears *did* know was that I wasn't going to talk. They never even *hoped* I would; it was as if something forced them to go through the motions anyway. Kind of like a dance, only with no music.

It was also a race with no winners.

The bears were racing to defuse one bomb, but all that time, I was busy building another. I even had a punch list, like the construction bosses always carried with them. I didn't have a yellow pad, or an aluminum box to keep it in, but I had a better place to store things.

Step One came naturally. The locals always get the first chance—not only do they know the territory best, they're already inside it before word reaches beyond their borders.

But this time, they knew they had to work fast, and that knowledge drove them something fierce. When you feel the Devil's own breath on the back of your neck, you can't even waste the energy it takes to turn around and see how close that hellhound is.

Even so, they couldn't just crash through the brush without worrying about how much noise they made. Knowing the territory best also meant everyone in that territory knew *them*, too.

They would have liked to have the hive completely surrounded before they made their move, but they didn't have that luxury. They had always been the top dogs here, but they knew that was due for a change.

And quick, too.

Bigger and more deadly bears were on their way; you could already feel the ground trembling under their weight. The locals knew they would never be able to drain the hive dry—the best they could hope for was to pull out anything that could hurt them before they were shoved out of the way.

Those bigger bears had no need to poke and probe and look for openings. They didn't have to pussyfoot around—no matter what popped out when they squeezed, nothing in that hive posed a danger to any of them.

Why be subtle when you don't care what kind of tracks you leave? When the bigger bears were all done squeezing, there'd be nothing left but a tiny little lump.

Just big enough to stick that goodbye needle in.

When you're arrested for murder, you don't have much to trade. The rule is, you have to trade *up*, like when a drug addict gives up his dealer. But if you've done *considerable* killing, talking about who paid you for those services might make the Law so happy that they'll spare your life in exchange. Or even turn you loose.

But once you get down to murder for money, the Law's not the only player at the table. No matter how high up those you talk to may stand, no matter what they promise, you know that even the *rumor* of you talking can end it all.

Once the Law has you like they had me, you *are* going to die.

There isn't but one actual option left to you, only one thing you can still control. You get to decide who does the job.

If you make the Law do it, all they can kill is your body. Your spirit lives, and your reputation carries on.

When you die the right way, there's no reason for anyone to seek vengeance on your loved ones.

Just the opposite, in fact.

The crime that finally brought me down made national news. But that was just because of the body count. National news doesn't always bring in national Law.

All the killings had been in one state, so there was no way the Feds could just ram their way in and take over. That's what the local Law kept telling themselves, anyway. They ran around saying "jurisdiction" to each other like it was a holy word . . . the way people in the movies hold up a cross to banish vampires.

That only works in the movies.

Keeping the Feds out of our business, that's like a religion around here. But if a federal agent gets killed—they *are* coming. Get in their way and, no matter how big you are, lawman or not, you're nothing but a pile of hot asphalt waiting on the steamroller.

All I could do was be patient. Deep inside, alone, watching the layers of protection I'd taken so many years to build up slowly come off.

I knew this would happen someday. I thought I was ready for it, because I'd had so much practice. When I knew pain was coming, I could go someplace in my mind. Someplace else. From there, I could watch it happening, happening to me, but I didn't feel it. I'd learned to do that as a child. Maybe not "learned," because I hadn't studied on it—one day, I realized it had just happened. After that, it always did.

And now it was happening again. I was watching what the big bears were watching. Only, this time, what they were watching was an illusion. They weren't getting any closer to what they really wanted. But the closer they thought they were getting, the easier it was for me to keep checking steps off my list.

It seemed like everyone in the world wanted to talk to me. But even if they weren't undercovers, they damn sure weren't showing up because they cared about me.

And I surely didn't need any "spokesman." There was no shortage of volunteers for *that* job.

I didn't worship "the media" the way most folks did. Longing for attention is for killers who *haven't* been caught. Like that Zodiac sex fiend in California who kept sending letters to the papers. Or that Unabomber psycho who wanted to see his stupid "manifesto" in print. Now he has the rest of his life to read it.

I'm nothing like them. I'm not crazy. I never wrote taunting notes to the police; I never got a thrill out of what I did. I was just an assassin, good at my trade. Like any skilled workman, I charged a fair wage for my work, and I never expected payment in full until I finished each job to the customer's satisfaction. Contract killers aren't all the same. The only thing we have in common is that we all commit murder for money. Speaking for myself, it was *only* for the money.

But there's more to this work than making people dead. The contracts always have other terms and conditions to them, and those hold forever. It didn't matter if I was caught—as long as I didn't cross those lines, I was free to strike any deal for myself that I could.

Only I didn't want a deal.

ust as the local bears got their first turn at me, the local boss bear—the District Attorney himself—took his before anyone else.

He came to the jail alone. Well, not really alone. He had a couple of assistants with him, and the Sheriff's men were real close by all the time. They weren't there to protect him; it was their job to bear witness to the act of Christian charity that the big boss was going to deliver.

When everybody was in place, he reached down and shook my hand.

"You'll never face the death penalty in this county, Esau," he said. "Folks around here, we all know what you've been through."

He never specified on that, but he sure as Satan knew why I hadn't stood up when he'd held out his hand.

I knew he would never try for the death penalty anyway. Not around here. Not for someone like me.

I'd read up on this, and I knew the defense could ask for a change of venue—that's moving the trial to another part of the state. But if I had planned on actually putting up a defense, I'd've never let that happen. I knew what the DA knew—no matter who they picked for the jury, as long as it was from folks around here, they'd never vote to execute me.

They'd never vote to elect that DA again, either. They take insults like that real personal around here.

That's why the words tumbled out of his mouth like a rolling bakery line of fresh lemon tarts, with a little strand of barbed wire hidden in each one.

I knew they'd come that way—you can't use a harpoon when you're fly-fishing.

But they kept using the wrong bait. I couldn't come right out and tell them what to use, either. I did that and they'd all think I was the one holding the casting rod.

'd known this time was coming. I'd known it for many years. The only excuse I had for the hive not being fixed up just right was that I hadn't planned on those other visitors—there wasn't any reason to expect them.

The design did just what it was supposed to do: the more the bears dug at it, the stronger the hive got. Pull off one layer and the others would fold in on themselves, only wrapped much tighter. I was sure I'd made that honey armor-plated.

But, like I said, I hadn't built it expecting the Feds. I had counted on never having to deal with them, because I'd been so careful to stay away from anything that might draw their attention.

It's not like TV. This place could be home base for a dozen serial killers, and still the local Law would never call on the Feds for help. Around here, you could be anything from a U.S. marshal to a census taker; you'd still be a Fed.

Nobody likes the Feds. That goes back a long way, and its roots are deep.

But I shouldn't have counted on all that to keep me safe.

tep Two kind of came by itself. Once the Feds took over, they acted just as smug and arrogant as you'd expect. Came straight out and said it, first words. Anything anyone in this whole state could do for me, the Feds could do better. A lot better.

They could even fix it so I'd never spend another night behind bars.

When the locals were trying to get me to hand over the honey, they called it "cooperating." That word tastes foul in the mouth, just saying it. Like collaborating with the enemy.

The Feds were much smoother. They called it "debriefing," like I'd been out on an undercover mission. That didn't taste as bad. If I'd been with them all along, all the talking they wanted me to do wouldn't be a killer pointing the finger at the people who'd hired him. No, it would be a special kind of federal agent, reporting in from the field.

They even said they'd get that put in the papers, so everyone would know what a hero I'd been.

I knew that what people would think of me had nothing to do with what they might read in the papers.

Maybe that's why the Feds can never get in deep enough—all they ever have is a bunch of paper reports. If they needed someone to infiltrate a terrorist network, they had to recruit one who was already inside. Never occurred to them that they should put their own terrorists out there, and let the networks recruit *them*.

It's not just that they aren't patient enough, they're too . . . disconnected, I guess is the best way to put it.

They know how to put their own people in with certain groups, but they can only pull it off when their agents are the same as the people in the group. White, I mean.

Maybe that's why it never crossed their minds that I might have killed some of those people for my own reasons.

At least the Feds were honest enough to tell me that they were determined to fill their basket, and they had a whole shopping list. But my name wasn't on it. Never been on it, they swore.

I did believe that last part.

When I say "Feds," I'm using that blanket to cover a whole slew of them. It seemed as if a new agency hatched every day. FBI, DEA, IRS, ATF . . . the only one they always called by its full name was Homeland Security.

Way too many of them to accomplish anything. All they did was get in each other's way. They kept telling me how they were all on the same side, but they kept going at each other like they were blood enemies . . . even right in front of me.

I started seeing them all the same way I do preachers: real good at telling other people how to act—but they had some special, private deal with God, so they were exempt from those same rules.

You want to buy yourself a real chance at salvation, well, you make sure you throw something in the collection plate. And chip in to buy the preacher his new car every year, too.

I guess it sounds like I hate men of the cloth. I don't, not really—I generally liked those I met personally. Except for the fat old swine who had hinted that what had happened to me and Tory-boy was God's punishment for some sin.

If any of the people I'd done work for had wanted that one killed, I would have given it to them cut-rate.

The more I thought about that man, the more hate came into me, like lungs gasping for air when you'd been underwater too long. Whatever sin had been committed didn't belong to me or Tory-boy. Anyone who couldn't see that was too dirty in his own mind to be allowed to call himself a man of God.

The way it ended with all those different Feds was when one of them told me that their task force was being disbanded because of "cooperation issues." That was pretty funny.

What happened was what always happens: the strongest bear drove the rest of them off.

You'd think that would be Homeland Security, but it was the FBI team who came out on top. Didn't even break a sweat doing it, either. It wasn't a blood-drawing fight; hardly a tussle, in fact. You could see who had the real muscle just by listening to them say "good morning" to each other.

ATF was the toughest to push out. They only left after telling the

FBI team that they "expected a complete report." But the way they said it, it was the same way some guys mumble threats under their breath as they're walking away after backing out of a fight.

Step Three was revealed to me as soon as they trimmed down to one agency. The FBI couldn't stop saying "RICO." They soft-spoke it, like it was sacred.

They told me I would be serving the people. Protecting thousands, all over the country. Doing the right thing.

One of the older agents even told me that giving them what they wanted was my only path to forgiveness.

I knew I was past any forgiveness. And if forgiveness was going to come from them, I didn't even want it. Had this same government that now was trying to make me talk done the right thing when it had the chance, none of this would have happened at all.

For that, I could never forgive *them*.

One of them was a black guy. He said if I told them everything I'd be a kind of savior. The people they wanted me to inform on were killing my community. Sucking the life out of it, parasites feeding on decent people. You could tell he hadn't done any more research about this place than looking it up on a map.

At first, nobody paid any real attention to me. They all had some routine they believed in, so that's what each one went with. None of them even waited to see if I was buying it, just kept talking. Talking and nodding to themselves . . . like senile old men do in nursing homes.

Finally, they stopped. All of them. Like they'd heard the same alarm clock go off.

The next morning, they all sat around in this horseshoe, forming a wall around me to the front and sides. My back was already against the wall, so I was surrounded.

They just sat there, waiting.

I moved my head around the horseshoe, so each and every one of them would know I was including him in my deliberate silence.

It was graveyard-quiet. I couldn't hear them breathe. I guess they misunderstood my message—if I was ready to open the floodgates, they wouldn't want to miss a drop.

So I went around the horseshoe with my eyes again. Even slower this time. I had every molecule of their attention.

"You know what's lower than a maggot?" I said. "That would be a man who informs on his own partners. Everyone on a job takes some kind of risk. But if you're caught, a man's meant to play his own hand."

"How do you think we found *you*, Mr. Till?" one of the agents said.

"I wouldn't know about that," I said, surprised it took them so long to try that sorry trick.

"You want it spelled out, we can do that," another one spoke up. "Would that do it? If we gave you the name of the man who gave us yours, would you be ready to—?"

I stomped on the hand he'd been using to deal the marked cards from the bottom of the deck. I'd known enough men who'd been through this same game before to know exactly what to say to them.

"If somebody gave you my name, why don't you just ask *him* what you want to know?"

They went quiet again. I let their silence settle before I said: "Sure. So you're either bluffing, or the guy you got was some little messenger boy. Like a FedEx driver who knows where he dropped off a package, but couldn't tell you what was in it, never mind who had it sent."

They just kept looking at me.

"Anybody you got to talk to you, he doesn't know anything," I said. "A guy like that, he wouldn't do any heavy lifting. All he's good for is sticking up gas stations, running errands, getting drunk, and beating his wife. Probably has a long enough sheet so another felony would put him under the jail."

Watching their eyes was like reading a newspaper.

"Sure . . . that's probably it. You got this guy—the one you say gave you my name—but you got him for something else, didn't you? Nothing to do with this other thing you keep asking me about.

"Maybe he had warrants out. Maybe he was already on parole. But whatever it was—if you're even telling me the truth—that would have been for his own crimes, not anyone else's. So he can't give you a thing. You could drill as deep as you wanted, you'd never hit a vein."

They still kept quiet. I guess it was some kind of technique: let me talk enough, maybe I'd drop something they could use.

That wasn't going to happen. But all that silence had already told me I was right, so there was no harm in telling them some more of what they already knew.

"A man like that, he'd tell you everything," I went on. "Spill his guts . . . if he had any to spill. Enough for a search warrant? Sure. But you already found enough stuff in my place to connect me to all kinds of things, didn't you? Your problem is, there's too much space between what you found and what you want. Especially what you want the most—names.

"So you used your computers. Probably, by now, you can tell each other you know who hired me. At least you think so. Only problem is, you can tell each other all you want, but you can't ever tell a jury."

An older guy with a short haircut—not like it was "styled" or anything, more like he didn't want to be bothered with going for haircuts too often, so he told them to take off as much as they could—he had one of those ripsaw voices. He didn't have to speak loud, because when he opened his mouth everybody else shut up.

"You have to admire a man who won't inform on his friends," he said. A jab, just to watch my response.

About ten seconds passed. When I still didn't say anything, he threw the sucker punch he'd been storing up all along.

"But the people we want aren't your friends," he said. "They aren't your 'partners,' like you called them. You're a hired hand. A day laborer. They don't think any more of you than someone they'd hire to cut their lawns. Or scrub out their toilets."

I looked in his eyes—twin flecks of the ground we have around here, dark brown and rock-hard.

"I know that," I told him.

That wasn't the answer he was expecting. His face didn't move a muscle, but I could feel the words hit him just the same.

But this guy was too much of a professional to be taken out with one punch.

"Then just tell me something, Esau," he said. "Tell me why a man with your intelligence wouldn't take this incredible opportunity. The opportunity we're offering you, right now, here, today. Can you tell me that much? Just for my own understanding."

My hands rested on the wheels of my chair. Rested lightly. "That's not how I roll," I told him.

And I smiled real friendly, so he'd know there was no hard feelings.

Later that night, alone in my cell, I thought about what I'd said. There's probably a lot of different ways to look at those parting words of mine.

Maybe the Feds had meetings about that; I don't know. As far as they were concerned, I guess those were my last words, in all respects.

But just because I'd turned down their best offer didn't mean they were going away. They couldn't do that: there was a fire to feed, a legend to maintain.

Kill a Fed and you die. You *all* die.

But lurking shadows don't scare me—I grew up under them.

So, when Step Four came out a shade of gray, I plucked it out right away.

Every bomb-builder has his own style, but there are certain rules for all: handle the ingredients with respectful delicacy, and never close it up until everything needed is inside.

That's why I never stopped talking with the Feds. They had one of the ingredients I needed before I could wrap the package.

Ever since I came to understand that money can buy more than just things—like cars or houses or big TVs—I'd gone after it. I committed all kinds of wrong acts for all kinds of wrong people, all purely for the money. The money to buy safety for me and Tory-boy.

I was all done with that kind of work, but I still needed money.

It wasn't just money I needed, it had to be *clean* money. I didn't care what they called it, or whose name was on whatever paper they signed to get it, but the money would have to come from a source the Feds couldn't ever trace back to those wrong people I had done all that wrong work for.

I knew the Feds would be watching any money coming in to me. And even if I managed my way around that, I'd have to get the money back out.

There's ways of informing without actually saying a word. There's ways you can draw a bright-red arrow pointing wherever you want it to. The people I'd worked for, they'd expect me to be aware of this.

So I had to make sure they knew I was keeping faith with them. Because now the river was flowing in the opposite direction. A certain kind of work still had to be done. But instead of getting paid, I was fixing to make some payments.

Maybe I should have said to myself, "Well, I was always loyal to them, why shouldn't they do this one last thing for me?"

But you don't ask favors of your employers. That's not the relationship. Nothing I had done for them had been an act of friendship. You might be friendly with a doctor, but you don't walk into his office without expecting a bill when you leave.

I never even considered the possibility. Even if they wouldn't think of it as blackmail—and I wouldn't blame them if they did—that's just not how it's done. I'd been paid fair and square for what I did, every time I did it. That's where the old saying comes from: "If you don't like the job, just put the bucket down." My kind of work means that you put it down *gently*, not drop it and splash water all over everyone else.

I'd had a goodly amount put away, in different places. But once they had locked me up, I'd been forced to spend a big chunk of that money.

Most of that went toward keeping things in place while I waited them all out. That wasn't so hard. I was used to doing business over the phone, and I could use the jailhouse pay phone anytime I wanted. After all, I hadn't been actually convicted of anything yet, so I was what they call a "pre-trial detainee," and that gives you certain rights.

And moving money you already had stashed away wasn't difficult at all—if the Feds couldn't watch it come in, they couldn't watch it leave. Which meant they couldn't see where it landed.

All I had to do was call certain people and tell them I was concerned about a project of mine: an ancient Ford I had found buried under a ton of garbage in this old barn that was on some property I'd purchased. That car was a pretty rare thing, especially because it still had the flathead V-8 it came with. I'd ask if they'd managed to find a certain part—like a fender or a headlight. For the people I called, those words were as easy to follow as a map.

Paying our way to keep everything in place, that had always been costly. But there had never been a shortage of work, so it hadn't been a real problem. In fact, even as expensive as certain things I'd needed had been, I'd still been able to put quite a bit aside.

But now that I couldn't work, there'd be no fresh money coming in, and no way to restock. I had to get my hands on one big chunk. No more installment plans for me; this one time, I had to buy what I wanted outright.

I knew one way I could transfer money so the Feds couldn't trace it in a thousand years, but that was something I could pull off only once.

The people I was never going to name knew the position I was in, but they still trusted me. The way they proved that was by staying away. If they hadn't trusted me, the first thing they would've done would've been to send in a lawyer. Only he wouldn't be my lawyer; he'd be theirs. A spy.

Had they done that, it would have hurt me deep. Might have insulted me enough to push me over to whatever side made me the best offer.

By keeping their distance, they freed me from that choice. Maybe that was a show of respect, or maybe it was nothing more than them knowing I'd never trust any lawyer they sent. No more than I'd ever trusted them.

But what it probably came down to was simple, brutal math: I might be holding some high cards, but they held the trump.

My little brother.

Step Five was kind of forced on me. Considering my income—all the government knew about was what I got from Disability—the judge said I couldn't afford a private lawyer. That meant the State had to give me one. In fact, they gave me two.

I didn't want any special treatment from some judge that I'd never met—that was pretty typical of the way strangers had looked at me all my life. Strangers from around here, I mean. A lot of people I'd never met still seemed to know who I was when we got introduced.

"Poor Esau," that's how I was looked upon. Not by way of money, but . . . the way I was born. What I was born with. The burdens I had to struggle with. I could feel them thinking how terrible that must be for me.

And how glad they were it wasn't *them* in that wheelchair.

But after I finished researching it, I realized that judge wasn't treating me special after all. I found out that the State always gives two lawyers to any indigent defendant in a capital case.

I only met with those State-paid lawyers one time. "The first thing you need to understand is that we can't do our job unless you're totally honest with us," I remember one saying before promising to come back in a few days.

Before that happened, another bunch of lawyers showed up. They were a private group, they told me. Like missionaries, traveling around the country. Only their mission wasn't to save souls from hellfire; it was to save bodies from the death penalty.

They left me a bunch of stuff to read, the way a vacuum-cleaner salesman leaves his "literature" with everyone who's not buying that day.

That was because I told them I wasn't going to take any prosecution deal. I was going to trial, no matter how heavy the prosecutor sweetened the pot. They really perked up at that—and worked hard at trying not to let me see it.

I knew what was in their minds. It wasn't that any of them expected me to be acquitted. But if I was going to trial, they had a good excuse to stick around. It was a capital case, after all. So even after—they said "if," but I knew they must say it that way to every client they ever had—I was found guilty, there would still be what they called the "penalty phase." And that was where they could outdo any court-appointed lawyers in the country, they told me.

That was where they were going to step in and save me. In the penalty phase, whatever I had done wouldn't be as important as why I did it. "That's the most critical factor, Esau," the girl they always brought with them told me. "We have to make the judge and the jury see you as an individual. They have to know who you are, from the inside out. Because the more they know you as a person, the less they'll be willing to . . . hand down the ultimate sentence."

She just went on and on. They were going to show the jury how I really didn't have any choice, the kind of life I'd had, blah-blah-blah.

They didn't know one single thing about any of that. All they knew was what anyone could see for themselves: I was born bad—the spine thing. They just assumed I was raised even worse, me being poor white trash, living on Disability, no education, no job, no prospects. "No hope," she said, like that was a knockout punch.

I'd rather take a bullet than pity, but how could these people know that? They didn't know me.

They didn't even know how dumb they sounded. How could they be such great lawyers in capital cases if they had so much experience with the penalty phase?

When I told them I *wanted* the death penalty, I thought they'd just pack up and go back to wherever they came from. Not a chance. They said that would be State-assisted suicide, and they weren't about to let that happen.

So I made it even clearer—they didn't have any choice about what *they'd* let happen or not. That was up to me, not them. I reminded them that they weren't my lawyers. I didn't hire them, so I couldn't fire them, but the court hadn't appointed them, either. And wasn't about to.

What I didn't tell them was that they reminded me of doctors standing around the bedside of a dying man, already counting up which of his organs they could salvage. I just told them to get lost.

They kind of smirked when I said that. Especially the girl. She was way younger than me, dressed a little flashier than people around here consider seemly. Smelled good, too. She came over to where I was and sat real close.

"The lawyers the State appointed for you have tried exactly three capital cases between the two of them," she said, like she was sharing a secret.

I just shrugged.

"Mr. Diamond has tried over one hundred capital cases," she said, her eyes getting all big and shiny over the man she was worshiping. "Only seven defendants were sentenced to death, and every one of those is still on appeal."

"They still won't even let him in the courtroom without my say-so," I told her.

"It's a question of qualifications, Esau. When the court hears—"

"You went to Yale, Brooke?" I interrupted her. I didn't even meet her eyes, just kept looking down at the sheet of paper with her name at the top. I wouldn't normally have ever talked to a woman like that; I pride myself on my manners. But when a girl half my age calls me by my first name, like I was a child instead of a grown man, I admit I resented that.

"Yes, but—"

"That's where you learned to be a lawyer?"

"Oh, no. Law school is where you learn the law. It's only down in the trenches where you learn how to practice it." She glanced over at this Diamond guy, hoping for any little nod of approval—the only stake she was really playing for.

"There's no trenches around here," I told her. "Just a lot of abandoned mines. I don't need your little lectures, okay? You don't know the people around here; I do. And the way they figure, if a man doesn't take the stand and deny he did something, that's the same as confessing to it."

"The State can't—"

"They can't *say* that's the reason, that's all. And, me, I'm not taking any stand, so . . ."

That's when her Mr. Diamond kind of strolled over and put his hand on the girl's shoulder. I thought she was going to swoon.

"It's too soon to make that kind of decision, Esau. Way too soon." He had one of those resonant voices, but he used it to talk down to me—like he was explaining something simple to someone even simpler.

I hadn't much cared for him before, but now I had a true dislike. Not just for treating me like I was slow, but for trying to tell me he was in charge. In charge of my life.

I didn't answer him. Just nailed his eyes until they dropped. Compared with other men I'd stared down, he was soft as custard.

There was another man on their team. He wasn't a lawyer, they were quick to tell me, to make sure I didn't mistake him for one of them. No, he was their investigator. The best in the business, they said.

This man was wearing a suit, but nobody would take him for a lawyer.

Black suit, white shirt, black tie. Nothing flashy, but anyone he approached, they'd know he was taking them seriously, coming at them respectfully.

He was a real tall, skinny guy. The minute he opened his mouth, I knew he was, well, not from around here, but from *around* around here, if you get what I mean. I could feel his eyes pulling at me while the boss was talking. I glanced over and I saw him shake his head. Not the way you do when you're saying "no" to someone, more like when you're feeling sorry for them.

I knew that look real well. Only he wasn't looking at me; he was looking at the great Mr. Diamond.

I think he must've said something to them later. I'm sure of it, actually. Because, the next time they came, everyone who spoke to me was careful to call me "Mr. Till."

I appreciated that not one bit—for them, it wasn't showing respect; it was just strategy. And it didn't change anything. Every fancy clump of words they peddled in front of me only added up to another No Sale.

Four days of them was way too much. But it had given me time to gather some information. They've got an Internet connection in the Sheriff's office—the jail is right behind it, in the same building—and the folks on the night shift were always nice enough to look up whatever I asked them after those lawyers had left for the day.

As soon as I had all the information about them that I wanted, I just told them: "Go find somebody who snatched a little girl, had his fun with her, then chopped her up. That's the kind of human garbage who'd want you all rushing in to save him from the chair. Or the needle, or whatever they use wherever he is."

At that, Mr. Diamond got up. Like that was a signal, they all did the same thing. He tossed a card on the little wood table in front of me, like one of those old *Have Gun—Will Travel* reruns me and Tory-boy used to watch all the time.

"If you ever change your mind, all you have to do is give us a call. We'll take care of everything from there."

He didn't call me by my name—first or last—when he said that. He didn't look back, either. Why would he? None of that whole display was aimed at me.

I left his card for the guards to pick up. Maybe one of them would find a use for it someday.

Every autumn, the trees blaze with color. When one of those fiery leaves falls to the ground, it holds on to its color for a while. But, even though you can't tell just by looking at it, that leaf's already dead.

That was me, that leaf. One way or another, I had lied to every one of those lawyers. It was always my plan to take the stand and testify. That was the only sure way I knew to tell the people who needed telling that I'd never tell on them.

It wasn't death itself I wished for. If that's all I'd wanted, I could have managed it on my own easy enough. What I wanted was the *sentence* of death. That would leave me in control long enough to make sure my last plan had gathered enough speed to keep rolling on its own without me pushing it from behind.

Staying alive in prison, that's not a sure thing. And I wouldn't have access to anything that would even up the odds. So I had to find the safest place to do my watching from.

The safest place in prison is Death Row.

That was the advantage of me knowing I was that still-fiery leaf. Lying on the ground, waiting for the weather to change. I knew *any* death-penalty case would drag out for years and years. It didn't matter if there was real doubt about a man's guilt, or none at all— one appeal after another was a sure thing.

Roger Lucas lived a few miles from where me and Tory-boy did. Roger killed a clerk who tried to stop him from robbing a convenience store. Then he went into the back of the place and killed the two other people he found there. Shot each of them in the head because he was worried they might have seen him shoot the clerk.

No one will ever know what they saw, but the security cameras didn't miss a thing. All that happened about fifteen years ago, and Roger Lucas is still waiting for his number to come up.

I'd never been in prison, but I knew plenty of men who had, and they'd all told me the same thing: if you were sick or weak or old, you'd be better off on Death Row than any other place in prison. It's the only way to guarantee you get a cell to yourself. And those cells, they're bigger and nicer than regular ones. If you've got the money, you can have a TV and order books and hobby-craft materials . . . all kinds of worthwhile stuff.

Even the guards were supposed to be pretty decent, as long as you weren't in there for some freakish crime. And if you were white, of course.

I took all that into consideration.

Even with all the crimes I was planning to admit to, I knew years and years would go by before they ever came for me. And with this disease I carry, my life was a two-horse race—the only question was which kind of death would cross the finish line first.

In fact, the more I think on it, the more I'm convinced that it was hearing that doctor tell me I was unlikely to ever see age fifty that had started this whole thing rolling.

I remember reading the dictionary when I was just a kid. I could only do it during the day back then, so I just skimmed it, looking for words that called to me.

"Inertia," that was my favorite of all. It means that once something starts rolling, it's going to keep rolling unless some stronger outside force stops it.

By the time I read that definition, I was already rolling myself. And nobody or nothing has stopped me since.

What I needed was to be gone.

Gone, but still around.

I'm the most patient man you'll ever meet. You learn patience when you have to do everything for yourself. When nothing about you past the end of your spine works, it takes a lot of time to do even the smallest things.

But it wasn't patience that kept me from killing myself. I needed folks to always say, "Esau Till didn't give it up; he made them come and get it."

If you leave that kind of name behind you, burned in deeper than anyone could ever chisel a tombstone, it counts for a lot.

Others have done so. And it spooks folks seriously whenever they hear their names said aloud.

I was pretty sure I knew how to make all that happen. The trick was to keep the lawyers away.

The free lawyers, that is. Some would be the kind who didn't care about the case, just the cause. Like that Mr. Diamond and his followers. They're so against the death penalty that they end up specializing in defending people who need killing.

You know the kind I'm talking about—those who kill just because they like doing it. Only makes sense that normal folks would enjoy killing *them*.

In fact, I was counting on that.

The other kind of free lawyer would be one of those you see on

TV all the time. "High-profile," they were called. Didn't matter if they won or lost, people would remember their names. Which was the whole point.

Problem with their kind is that you lose all control. No telling what they'd say when they went in front of the camera.

Besides, it wasn't their name I needed people to remember, it was *mine*.

All my life, I gathered up information like I was harvesting a crop. A man who buys a pistol may never have to pull the trigger, but it comforts him to carry it around. Some places more than others.

Every piece of information I gathered, I tested, every chance I got. If it didn't qualify as reliable, it didn't qualify as information.

That's why I knew so much about Death Row. The first man to tell me about it, his brother was there at the time. When he told me that some of those men have fans—I mean, like a movie star might have—I didn't believe him. But enough other folks said the same thing that I eventually came to accept it.

Serial killers, especially the ones who killed girls, they had women wanting to marry them. That's the truth, too, although I never believed it until I started getting those same kind of letters myself.

I surely had a high enough body count to qualify as a serial killer and mass murderer, both. But I didn't need any fans; I needed money. Real money, not some twenty-five-dollar money order so I could have pictures of myself taken to mail back to them.

Step Six was a tumbler falling into place. You couldn't see it with your eyes; you couldn't hear it without a stethoscope—but if you'd worked with locks enough, you could feel it.

The Feds proved they had the money, all right. Tons of it. But they weren't getting up off one dime unless I gave them information. Hard information. The kind that would get me a lot of company in the Death House.

Oh, they could see easily enough that I wasn't afraid of dying. That shook them a little at first, but not all that much. They had studied how to make people tell them things. That's why they kept upping the offer, but always held it just out of my reach, like taunting a dog to jump higher if he *really* wanted the bone.

That might be a useful tactic against most killers, but it was doomed against me. The Feds never did understand what *would* have worked. And I would have died a thousand times before I'd ever let them know.

If they'd ever known what button to push, I would have sung like a whole aviary. But what they had wouldn't draw a peep from a born canary.

"This is the way it works," one of them told me. "You give us something. Not everything we want, not at first, but some little piece of it. We check it out. If it turns out you're being truthful with us, then we release a little piece of what you want. That's only fair, right?"

I didn't answer him. I already had that bad feeling you get inside you when you know a promise is a lie. A girl's smile, a man's word—it doesn't matter—there were times when you just knew they wouldn't ever prove true.

"Then you turn over a little bigger piece," the Fed went on. "And we get you a bigger chunk of the money. It can go as high as you take it, Esau—Uncle Sam's got all the money there is."

I think he knew all along I wasn't going to do any trading with him, but it was his job to try, so he kept at it.

Just like that dog who couldn't quite manage to grab that taunting bone.

Step Seven came after days of their useless hammering, as if I didn't understand that the Feds weren't going to give me the money I needed without me giving certain people up first.

I didn't panic. I still had money enough to make certain nobody bothered Tory-boy for quite a while. And if there's one thing I know how to do, it's wait.

I was almost three months behind bars before someone who had all the money I needed showed up. I hadn't reached out for him. I wouldn't have even known where to look. He just came.

He had the money, all right. But he was a man who was used to being accommodated. He said they—he meant the TV people he fronted for—they wanted to put me in front of a camera. Kind of like an acting job, he said. They'd call it an "interview." I'd have to pretend some plastic-faced fool had broken me down, sliced me open with his scalpel-sharp questions, then pulled back the skin to show everyone the truth underneath.

Since I was planning to tell a pack of lies in court anyway, I couldn't see any harm in repeating them on camera. And the money man didn't care, either . . . just as long as I told *his* people first.

But even with clean money coming in, I would still need one thing only the Feds could give me. And I couldn't let them know how bad I had to have that one thing, or they'd have me on a steel leash.

I worked it over and over again in my mind, trying to strengthen it, the same way you do with a muscle. And, sure enough, I came up with a perfect package. All the while the Feds were working so hard trying to find out what I wanted, what would make me talk, they were busy telling me what *they* wanted.

I don't mean who paid me to do what, I mean that special piece. The one they wanted *bad*. All I had to do was listen.

Step Eight came when I realized I could give the Feds what I knew they wanted more than anything else, and *still* keep faith with the people who had hired me for all the jobs I was never going to talk about.

A simple formula: if I could just get the right lies accepted by one side, that would prove my word was good to the other.

But that formula was easier to memorize than put into practice. For that, I had to move the TV man off his square—and he was standing his ground like a mother badger with cubs behind her.

"Esau, you don't have to tell us a thing about the crime itself. If you just talk about your life, what happened when you were just a little kid, how you raised your younger brother all by yourself . . . well, that alone could be worth the kind of money you've been asking for."

I didn't like that word "could." I wasn't about to be giving *them* enough leverage to keep raising the bar, either. And they weren't going for any kind of money-in-front deal.

So I had to sell them. And I knew that the only way that ever works is if the other man thinks he's selling you.

A *Life Story: As Told from Death Row,* they wanted to call it. It kind of disgusted me, but the TV people outbid all comers, even one of those newspapers that have stuff like two-headed monkeys on their front page.

I thought I had milked it as dry as I could, but when they learned I was going to the same Death House that had once held the Beast, that started them slobbering like dogs watching a butcher cut up a side of beef. Everything changed, then.

Still, the TV people held their place, made sure they were the last bidder standing.

So I told them that I'd go along but I had one little extra condition. That must have scared them a bit—I could see the relief spread over their faces when I spelled it out. The one extra condition was that they had to pay all the money direct into a trust I had already set up for Tory-boy.

So I was going to do it. Sit in front of their cameras as long as they wanted, and spin out the same lies I was planning to tell in court.

I was already inside my own balance when I finally made the deal. That's my lord and savior, balance. If that revelation hadn't come to me long ago, I wouldn't be waiting on my own execution as I write this down.

That's why I cleared all those lies I was planning to tell the TV people with the Feds. They weren't happy about it, but they went along . . . provided I didn't change what I was going to say on the witness stand.

I was almost done. Still, I knew I had to keep everything in balance, right to the end.

Step Nine was a surprise. That's when I *really* called on my balance. I had no choice—the negotiations hit a snag. Put straight up, I just couldn't risk the TV people editing what I was going to say. And they couldn't risk putting me on live, since they had to pay all that money into the trust before I said one word in front of a camera.

We stayed stalemated, with the clock ticking down. Finally, I saw a way to lure them in. I sifted through a giant pile of garbage at rocket speed. Easy enough, because I knew exactly what I needed: an investigative reporter. Almost all of those were entertainment puffers or celebrity snoopers, so there weren't but a few *real* possibilities.

I picked a guy who had a long track record of exposing things, bringing them to light. He'd just won a Pulitzer Prize for a story about a fearsome disease that actually could be prevented except that the vaccine wasn't carried by most doctors. In fact, it wasn't even mentioned by the medical people, all the way up to the Surgeon General's office.

Shingles, that was the disease. If you'd had chicken pox as a child—and most do—you were at risk for getting the shingles later on. The older you were, the greater the risk. Shingles can cause horrible pain. It's a kind of herpes; causes a rash that's so distinctive they can make the diagnosis just by looking at it. If you're unlucky enough that the rash reaches your face, you could even lose an eye.

And there's a vaccine to protect against it. A vaccine nobody ever talks about. Not even those giant national organizations that claim they're representing the elderly.

Everybody over sixty should be vaccinated, the same as they do for the flu, or pneumonia. And even if you had the shingles and it got cured, a vaccination could keep it from coming back.

So how come they kept this vaccine such a secret? It was this simple: Medicaid wouldn't always reimburse doctors for using it. Some insurance companies wouldn't pay for it, either.

Pure logic doesn't leave room for feelings. To a doctor, "heart" is an organ that pumps blood. If he isn't going to be guaranteed payment for doing some medical procedure—around here, you spell that "Medicaid"—he's not doing it.

A cliché never takes hold unless it had some traction to start with. Like the hillbillies with bad teeth you see in horror movies—Medicaid doesn't pay for dental work. And meth isn't exactly a cavity fighter, either.

When this reporter—Victor Trey was his name—broke the story, it was like the shingles rash breaking out on the government's own skin. They took so much heat that Congress ran in and changed the Medicaid law faster than they'd take a bribe. When I read that, I knew Mr. Trey was the man for what I had in mind.

I wrote him a letter—he didn't come across as a man who had a secretary to open his mail for him, especially a handwritten letter with a jail for a return address.

And I was right. Mr. Trey came all the way from California to talk to me. He tried to tell me about journalism ethics, protecting sources, stuff like that. I told him none of that meant anything to me—I'd asked him to come and visit with me because I had to find a reporter with a national audience who was also a reporter I could trust.

"What could I possibly give you but my word?" he asked me.

"A man's no better than his word," I told him. "I have to make a big bet. The biggest bet a man can make. I asked you to come here so I could make that decision."

He looked at me for a long time. Then he said, "You've done this before."

"Done what before?"

"Read people. Looked for dishonesty tells. Took the measure of another person by more than just his words."

I just nodded. He was the man I wanted, all right. I told him my plan.

I gave Mr. Trey the whole story. And it was a story—the exact same one I was going to tell on TV, in court, and anyplace else where I got asked.

Our agreement was that he'd run the story in what he called the "bulldog edition" of his newspaper. The show would air from nine to eleven at night—the bulldog would go out at midnight, in print and on the Web.

I guaranteed Mr. Trey he'd be the only print reporter I'd ever talk to. And he guaranteed me that no editor was going to touch what he wrote. So, if the TV people played it loose with their editing, they'd look like fools. And liars.

Mr. Trey and I shook on that. There isn't any more that could have been done, although he offered to put everything in writing.

"What would I do with a contract between men like us?" I told him. "For me, my word is a contract. Otherwise, I couldn't have done a lot of things I'm going to tell you about. I'm taking your word the same as mine was taken."

The next day, I told the TV people I'd let them bring their cameras in. They could ask me any questions they wanted, except for what I told them in advance was off-limits. I'd made sure they put that in the contract we all signed. Taking *their* word would put them in a class where they didn't belong.

I already knew I wouldn't have to answer the questions that frightened me to even think about—it would never occur to people like them to ask such questions. And the contract said they couldn't "go beyond the scope" of my crimes. No backstory, no digging into my life. I was a little concerned they'd balk at that part, but it didn't seem to bother them one bit.

"It's actually a better story this way," one of the TV big shots said to some of the others. He was talking about me like I wasn't in the room, but I wasn't insulted. The more invisible I could be, the more they'd say in front of me.

"Our audience is going to hear the story of a hired killer," the big shot said. "A detailed account of every murder. It's going to chill people's blood. You want to know why? Because we're not showing them some filthy, slobbering psycho; Esau looks like a college professor. That's the best part. Esau killed a lot of people because he got paid to do it. There's nothing more to the story. How scary is *that*?

"Serial killers, by now they're . . . they're almost boring. But what we've got is something truly unique—a pure predator. Not someone who kills because he's sick; someone who kills to feed his family. Every crime he talks about, the facts are right there for anyone to check. And the bodies are always going to be right where he says they are.

"See the beauty of it? If the competition wants to speculate on how Esau came to be what he is, that's fine with us. In fact, it's *better* than fine. Every time they interview some expert, every time they 'investigate' Esau's real motivation, they're promoting *our* product. I'll bet we sell more DVDs of this show than of all the rest we ever did, combined. It's going to be in criminology classes. Libraries. Cited in textbooks.

"You can't buy that kind of credibility. It's not only going to enhance our network image, win us all kinds of awards—it could turn out to have the longest legs ever."

You could see it on their faces. Even smell it coming off them like a thick, rolling fog of musk. To the other people in that room, what that big shot was saying was more important than oxygen.

With that in hand, I went on to Step Ten.

f everybody keeps up their end of the deal, I'll die alone. Alone and silent, the way I'm supposed to.

To the newspapers, I'll be the worst murderer in the whole history of this state.

I guess they should say that. I will have saved Tory-boy by telling the truth. A kind of truth, anyway. The kind of truth the Law feeds on. Once I learned how deep the Feds had their people planted in so many places, I had only one choice if I wanted to keep Tory-boy safe past my time.

The way I explained it was: I'd give all the politicians the truth-plus, if they'd agree to let it also be the truth-minus.

At first, there were some little disputes about who was going to have to kill me. I balanced it out for them: I told the Feds I could get the State to agree to push the buttons to send the poison through the IVs into what was left of my body.

I just came right on out with it: I'd clean up any unsolved murders on the State's books. If they'd allow me to come home to die, I'd use the mouth of one devil to make a lot of heroes.

And if the Feds had any other undercovers close by who'd met with death, I'd take those on myself, too.

What politician would turn down an offer like that?

And what lawman ever got to tell a politician what to do?

I kept my bargain. I confessed to every unsolved killing on the State books. Every killing I *could* have done, that is. Nobody was going to believe I raped a woman or kidnapped a child, or beat a man to death with a tire iron. The real truth is, I didn't want my name associated with such things, so I was deeply grateful when the Law agreed—they didn't want any taint on the big piece of paper they were going to roll out for the whole world to see.

When you took those kind of crimes out of the mix, you left a bunch of contract kills. The Law actually knew who did some of those—or ordered them, anyway—but they couldn't hope to prove it. And it turned out that the Feds had people planted all over the place. So, when I confessed to those crimes, I made everybody happy.

I had to walk that last bit of the line with great care. Confessing to a crime you didn't commit is tricky, because you don't know the little details—things only the killer would know.

Like that little red ribbon tied to a branch of the white-oak tree where a hunter had waited for hours before he put a 30.06 round through the head of a man named Luther Semple.

The Law *had* to know who shot him. Luther Semple had raped a little girl, but she couldn't identify him. She wasn't even the first little girl he had taken that way: throwing a feedbag over her head from behind before he went to work.

The cops were in a bad position. Everyone in that little town probably thought they knew who had fired the shot, and the little girl's father never denied it—just told the cops he wanted a lawyer and wouldn't speak to them at all.

The local prosecutor wouldn't touch the case. If he had, people would have looked at him as if he was the defense attorney for the rapist.

Still, nobody likes an unsolved murder. I don't mean "nobody" the way you'd talk about actual people; I mean "nobody" the same as the statistics the government keeps on everything. So, when I admitted that I'd killed that man, everybody was pleased. Me knowing about that piece of red ribbon, that was the clincher—even skeptical folks would have to admit that only the actual killer could have known that; it had never been made public.

But it wasn't all as easy as I'm making it sound. The way it worked was that the Feds would take all my confessions, then they'd call in the Law from whatever area the different crimes had happened in.

When those cops showed up, they'd be smart enough to get certain details out of me, so I could tell a straight story . . . but that's as far as they went. I damn near ended up telling them they were being stupid. Knowing a few facts just wouldn't be enough. The story had to ring true. How was a man in a wheelchair supposed to get into the deep woods? And why would I give a damn about somebody's little girl getting raped when I didn't even know them?

It reminded me of when I gave the Beast a story to tell the cops. I didn't just give him a version that sounded good, or that he wanted to be true. No, I planted it so deep in his mind that it even *felt* real.

So what I told those cops was this: I've got a rifle I built myself. The wheelchair is a natural brace to hold me steady, especially with its entire back made out of three-quarter-inch steel, and I could assemble the tripod by myself by just touching a push button. Any little flicker of doubt they might have had, I erased by telling them where they could find the whole apparatus. I hadn't even told the Feds that part. I could see in the eyes of the state cops how much they appreciated that.

I also told them that I was a dead shot—I could take a man at a hundred yards as easy as if he was sitting across from me. They didn't doubt that part.

I already knew that Luther Semple had been killed at a bit more than that distance. He was just sitting on his front porch, having a smoke, like he was pondering some big problem. He was tilted back, relaxing in his big chair, when his head exploded.

I knew more about that particular killing than anyone could imagine. I almost laughed out loud, confessing the truth to cops who were sure I was lying.

I wasn't lying. In fact, I had details they didn't have . . . but not the kind I'd ever speak of. The rifle I'd built was double-barreled with the scope mounted between them, chambered for .220 Swift. I hand-load all my ammunition, and that includes casting the slugs. If one of my home-built slugs hits you anywhere, you're not going to live long enough to get to a hospital.

There's almost no recoil, but that wasn't why I picked that cartridge—my legs are worthless, but my shoulders are like a pro linebacker's. The reason Luther Semple's head had exploded was the micro-warhead I had cast into the heart of the first slug.

My second shot was a hardball I always used as a make-sure. But the exit wound from the first was so big that the second slug went right on through, all the way into the woods behind his house. It was never found.

And it never would be. I don't know what it cost, but the man who'd hired me not only had that slug cut out of a tree, the same tree had been gas-fired right afterwards. I know who got that done, because the intact slug was turned over to me. That was how the man who'd hired me proved he was never going to betray me—he dropped the proof right into my hand.

He never did explain why he wanted that man dead, and I never asked.

The police report said Luther Semple had been ambushed by someone using a 30.06. That was an estimate, of course—the coroner's jury was told the slug was never recovered.

When the prosecutor from that little town drove down, he

wanted to interview me, too. All he really wanted to know was why I'd killed that man. I told him it was over a gambling debt. Three thousand dollars.

It's common knowledge that there are poker parlors around here, and the man who hired me had a dozen people ready to swear they'd been present when I won all Luther Semple's money. They particularly remembered that time because I'd been such a gentleman, taking his marker when he wanted to keep on playing. That's the kind of thing you just don't see much anymore.

So the man owed me money, and he wouldn't pay. Even laughed in my face: what was I going to do about it, chase him down in my wheelchair? Plenty of witnesses heard him say *that,* too.

Since I'd already confessed to quite a number of other killings, that story worked for everyone.

Everybody knew: Esau Till, he was one seriously vengeful man. If he'd take your life just for *looking* at him wrong, think of what he'd do if you *did* him wrong.

My court confessions were part of a deal—a patchwork quilt, big and warm enough to cover everyone who needed to climb under it. But I made sure to weave a pull-thread into that quilt. I put that part in about shooting Luther Semple because I did plead guilty to it, and anyone reading this needs to be able to separate which crimes I actually did from those I confessed to. So, if you're reading this, and you wonder why a contract killer would do such a thing, you'll know that confession was a real one.

There's nothing noble about any of this—what I'm writing now, I mean. I didn't write a word until I was sure that nothing I might put down could hurt the only people I ever cared about. You'll know who those people are soon enough.

But I do want vengeance. And I don't want anyone to think otherwise. Whether you speak a promise or a threat, it's still giving your word. And I never broke mine.

Step Eleven was nearly the last. When I finally got enough to make a *real* big pot, I anted it up, every dime. When I slapped it down on the felt, it wasn't to show off—it was to tell them to cut it right down the middle. All of it. I wasn't there when that was done, but the boss of each outfit was.

It was a ton of money, but it came with one condition attached: if either of them spent so much as a dime on anything but what we'd agreed on, then the other side would get my records.

Those records weren't going to send anyone to prison, but they would give the outfit that got them a big edge over the other one. Maybe even big enough to take over their territory.

That would be fine with me. If only one outfit failed me, I *wanted* the other one to be stronger, the better to keep Tory-boy safe. It didn't matter to me which outfit did whatever had to be done.

And if they both failed, if they both cheated me, I couldn't do anything about it. Except get even with them, and they knew I *would* do that.

Some people are born under misfortune, some travel a good distance to get there.

I was giving each boss a chance to choose his own fate. Not many get that opportunity.

They knew if the Law ever saw my records the State would have to build a whole new Death House—the one I'm in now is just about full up.

But which Law am I talking about? When I first came up with this idea to keep protection on Tory-boy, I wasn't sure which agency should get my records if word wasn't kept. But when I saw how just saying "RICO" got the FBI people so excited, that's when I knew.

There's a fairness to picking the FBI as well. If it hadn't been for them, I never would have been caught.

If they do get this, how they use it, that's up to them. I know they can't just show it to a judge to get a bunch of warrants. They do that and later on some slick defense lawyer is going to get to look at *all* of it.

And if that were to happen, dozens of closed cases would suddenly get unclosed. Cold cases the FBI claimed it had solved would turn into even colder ones. Promotions would get rescinded. Reputations would get unmade. And every agent who reached a higher post from all that stuff I confessed to would turn into a leper overnight.

That's why there's a copy. Of everything. And other hands are already holding it. I don't give a damn for anyone on the government's side of the line. No matter what they call themselves, they're still the government. And it was the government—every lousy part of it—that looked away from things that shouldn't have happened at all. Not to me, not to anyone.

So, even if the FBI does end up with my records, I know what they'll do with it. Same thing the government did with me. And my brother. And our sister, Rory-Anne—our mother. They'll razor out the parts they don't want known, and pay somebody to take care of the rest.

If that happens, the world will learn I was ready for it.

I don't know who'll be passing final judgment on any of the people in my story—I guess that depends on whether anyone ever gets to read this. "Final judgment" in a court, I mean. I don't know if there's a Heaven or a Hell or any of that.

I guess I'll find out, soon enough.

Or maybe I already have.

You'll see Step Twelve by the time you get to the end of this. Then you'll know that my "last word" wasn't the kind you put in a will. It was a threat. And you'll see I made good on it.

The back door I built years ago would always stay in place. If either boss failed to watch out for Tory-boy like each had sworn he would, I'd expect the other one to take over the job himself, even if that meant doing work in the other man's territory.

That's because it wouldn't *be* the other man's territory, not anymore. With the package the other one would be getting, he'd be taking over the whole town. Inside, he'd find all the other boss's contacts, from cops to politicians to the judges they put on the bench. All the murders, bought and paid for. All the inside businesses, from taverns to gambling joints to whorehouses. All the street businesses, from drugs to numbers. Where they got their guns, and where they kept their arsenals.

With that knowledge, nobody would be able to stop the man who held it. Not anyone from around here, and not anyone who tried to move in.

Two separate packages, one for each boss. That way, only the boss who broke his word would be at risk. And the other one wouldn't need to know anything about me or my life to do the job I left to him.

I believed that that boss, whoever he might turn out to be, would do exactly what was promised. He'd have to know there was another package, one I could still have delivered.

But you'd have to be from around here to understand that there was something far more potent than any poison cloud of information hovering over the people I had worked for.

Folks around here know death isn't always the end of the story. Some people come back. Good people, bad people—that piece of it doesn't seem to matter.

When I say "come back," I don't mean coming back to life. That doesn't happen. What comes back are spirits. You can't see them or touch them, but you know they're still around.

And nobody wants their attention.

Outsiders could never understand this, but if I died while still keeping certain names from coming out of my mouth, those I protected by doing so would owe me a debt—a debt of honor. If they didn't do what they had promised, they could never be sure I wouldn't come right out of my grave. If there's a God, even He'd know I'd had good reason.

Yqu've come this far, why not go the rest of the way? Make your own judgments of me. I know you won't all decide the same. And I truly don't care.

But *your* God . . . He just might.

From the beginning, anyone could take just one look at me and know I was born bad.

Spina bifida. You get born with it. That's why they call it "congenital," because it comes right along with your body as it leaves the womb. That whole network of nerves which branch out from the end of your spine never gets fully developed.

I never got told those words. Doctors don't talk to children around here; they only speak to parents. To the Beast, it was just "that spine thing."

It's a sorry world when a child has to look up his own disease in a book. I read everything I could find about it. When I came across speculation that there might be a genetic component involved, I let my eyes slide over those words.

I even learned there's ways you can help prevent it—the woman who's carrying the fetus can, I mean. Folic acid is best. You can make sure you have it in your diet, or even buy pills in one of those vitamin stores.

Not much brings a smile to my face, but the thought of Rory-Anne changing her diet so she could make healthier babies made me laugh inside.

What she should've done was have abortions. Probably would have, too. But she wasn't allowed—the Beast wasn't going to lose out on any of the money the government paid Rory-Anne to look after us.

Ever since I can remember, I've been able to go away. Not walk away. And I sure couldn't run. I mean, go away in my head. I saw things happen to Rory-Anne. I saw things happen to me. But it was all like watching some hideous horror movie—it terrified me, but I didn't actually feel any of it.

It's not that I can't feel pain. All that spinal thing did was numb me up pretty good downstairs. But the Beast knew he could hurt me, and that was real important to him.

He'd punch me in my chest, backhand me across the mouth, stuff like that. But even though I could see the blood and the marks later on, I never felt anything while he was doing it to me. It was like I was floating above, watching it happen.

It wasn't only the Beast. One time, Rory-Anne told me she was going to teach me to mind her. I didn't know what she meant, but I could hear the evilness in her voice.

I watched her drag my chair over to the stove and hold my hand over the flame. It must have hurt—the skin on the back of my hand came right off—but I didn't feel that, either.

When she saw what my hand looked like, Rory-Anne got scared. She picked me out of my chair and threw me in her car. All the way to the hospital, she warned me what she'd do to me if I told. I was to say I accidentally fell against the stove when my wheelchair skidded, and I couldn't move away from the fire.

So that was the story I told. At the hospital, they made such a big fuss over me that I wished I could stay there forever. And I could see they didn't want to turn me loose, either. Not because of the way they looked at me, because of the way they looked at Rory-Anne.

All that happened before Tory-boy came.

Tory-boy came and changed the world. My world, I mean.

Later, I learned how my life might have turned out different. When I was first born, Rory-Anne wouldn't claim me. The way I understand it, when she was told about the spine thing and all the special care I'd need, she just walked right out of the hospital, leaving me there.

It took a while for the government people to locate Rory-Anne, so the people at the hospital had to name me themselves. By the time they carried me to where Rory-Anne lived with the Beast, my birth certificate read "Esau."

Naturally, Rory-Anne had never told them who my father was. They had to put something down on the birth certificate, so they used Rory-Anne's last name.

Branding me with the mark of the Beast.

Some folks thought the Beast was doing a charitable thing, keeping me home after Rory-Anne had tried to abandon me. But most knew better than that. They knew he'd found out that a baby born as crippled as I was could fetch even more government money than a common Welfare child.

Rory-Anne never got over hating me—never tired of telling me what an ugly, twisted thing I was. But Tory-boy was different. He was born so big and beautiful that the nurses said he looked like a little prince. They even took him in to show Rory-Anne, told her how lucky she was.

So Rory-Anne not only claimed her second child; she even named him after herself.

It wasn't until a couple of years had passed that anyone knew Tory-boy was born as deeply cursed as me, only in a different way.

No matter how bad things ever got after Tory-boy came, I always managed to keep things in balance. Not the perfect balance I learned later on, but close enough so that we could get by.

"Getting by" is one of those sayings everybody uses. But those words mean different things to different people.

For me, they meant I had to keep me and Tory-boy alive until I could find a way to get us both out.

Tory-boy never could understand complications. For him, having our own place, that was everything. He didn't care what the furniture looked like, or if we had a big-screen TV or a microwave. Tory-boy never did covet things. But *feelings,* they were precious to him. And the most precious feeling of all was feeling safe.

What Tory-boy prized above everything on earth was the knowledge that nobody was going to wake him up in the middle of the night and start hurting him.

He probably thought that first little trailer of ours was magic. Oh, how he loved just hearing me say the words "our place." I could see it on his face every time I said it. Like I was casting a spell to keep us safe.

After a while, he started saying it himself.

Tory-boy wouldn't ever be able to understand how all this had happened, how it started way before he was even born.

I never burdened his mind with what I knew. Letting him

believe in magic worked just as good. Better, really. There are things no child needs to know.

Magic soothed Tory-boy, just as logic did for me. I don't remember the exact day, but I remember the feeling when it hit me, like an invisible lightning bolt striking deep inside my body.

From that moment on, I knew. It didn't matter what road map you followed: magic and logic would take you to the same place.

Place, that was the key. It's not the place you live in that keeps you safe; what keeps you safe is your place in the world.

Understanding how something works isn't enough. If you want to master it, be in complete control, first you have to take it apart . . . all the way down to its smallest component. Then you examine each separate piece to learn how they all fit together to form a functioning unit.

Doesn't matter if it's a grandfather clock or a criminal organization, the same rule applies—once you truly understand how things work, you can make them *stop* working.

I can do that. All of it. And I don't say this lightly. I taught myself, and I tested myself. Over and over again.

I had no other option. I knew I had to pass every test. So I stayed on every new one that popped up, like a barn owl who'd just spotted a mouse.

Getting it right once isn't worth a thing. That's the difference between validity and reliability. If you add x and y, and get z *one* time, then z is a valid answer. But if *every* time you add x and y you get z, then z is a reliable answer.

There's no higher honor for a man than a reputation for reliability—folks saying that you can always be counted on. In my world, it didn't matter whether folks said that about you in admiration or in fear. When they saw you coming, it didn't matter if they ran over to greet you or ran to get out of your way.

You aren't what people call you; you are what you do. What people *know* you can do.

So, when I say you need a place of your own to be safe, I'm not talking about some piece of ground. You can't make something your own with a title or a deed. The only things that are really and truly yours are those that can't be taken away. Being safe isn't about keeping people out; it's about bringing them in.

Bringing them inside a place you control. If they act right, it doesn't matter if they think they were invited in or just couldn't be kept out. It's only if they act wrong that they learn the truth.

You can't inherit a safe place; it's something you have to make for yourself.

That's the way the world works—and not just around here, either. If people don't need you for something, then they don't need you at all.

I'm not talking about some task you might be able to do, like washing their car or painting their house—that's not needing you; that's needing a job done.

Needing *you*, that's different. Reliability is the foundation to that. They not only have to need you, they have to count on you.

If people don't need you, there's no such thing as a safe place.

Plenty of people might have a use for you, but all that does is get you used up. It's only *while* they need you that you're in that safe place.

Just because people can count on you doesn't mean you can count on them. I once read that the definition of insanity is to act against your own self-interest. If that's true, I guess the definition of stupidity is not to know your own self-interest.

So you can never be sure of but one thing: sooner or later, you are going to get used up. Why people think they don't need you anymore doesn't matter. Any safe place you find, it's temporary, not permanent. That's why you always need the next place picked out in advance.

Most folks wouldn't understand how Death Row could be the safest place on earth. Not just for me—for Tory-boy, too. Every minute I stayed alive, he was safe.

It was what came after I was gone that I fretted so much about. But once I had my plans, I tested them in my mind, over and over again. It wasn't until I knew I could truly rely on them that I was finally at peace.

They always let Tory-boy visit me in the jail. The good folks around here, they might have lynched the Sheriff if he had barred that sweet, slow boy from visiting his crazy, crippled big brother.

Besides, the Sheriff worked for the same people I did, and he wasn't the kind of man who could live on his salary.

"Esau, I'm scared," Tory-boy whispered to me.

"What have you got to be scared of? Didn't I tell you our house was always going to be safe?"

"I know. But . . . who's going to tell me what to do now?"

"Me. I am."

"But people say you're going to . . ."

"Die? You can say it out loud, Tory-boy. It's not a spell-word. It won't come true just because you say it. I promise."

Those last two words had been soothing him since he was a baby, and they had never failed to do so. "All right, Esau. Do you want me to—?"

I held my finger to my lips. He knew that signal before he could talk.

I didn't like the way Tory-boy had been sneaking looks around the room where they let us have visits. I knew what was growing in his mind. Tory-boy can't think more than an hour or so ahead, but inside of that hour, he could clamp down on any one thing. Clamp down and *hold*.

I could see his mind: *There's no guard near us. They don't even lock the door behind me. Only one man on the desk in front. I can hit him hard. Then I can wheel Esau right out and put him in the van. We can go back to our place.*

"I don't want to get out of here." I knew saying that wouldn't frighten Tory-boy—he was used to me reading his thoughts.

"But . . . but you always say there's a way out, Esau. Like our secret mine, right? We can go home, and get right down there, like you said we might have to do someday—right, Esau?"

"I'm not going to die," I promised my big, powerful, life-cheated little brother. "Not until *I* decide to."

Tory-boy nodded. I'd never need to tell him that again. If I said it, Tory-boy knew it was true. And once Tory-boy had something from me, King Kong couldn't make him turn loose of it.

"I'm just going to another place," I told him. "You can come and see me there, too."

"Don't you want to come home, Esau? To our place?"

"Not yet. My plan is going to take years to work. In the meantime, I need a quiet place to think, so I can make more plans."

I could see by his face that he didn't understand. But I never get impatient. And I knew just what to do.

"'Our place.' Say it with me again, Tory-boy."

"Our place," we said together.

"Our place is always safe, isn't that true? Nobody ever hurt us in our place, isn't that the truth?"

"Yes, Esau."

"Well, I have to stay here for a while to keep it that way. It's part of the spell. This is one hungry spell, Tory-boy; I've got to keep it fed. Remember how I taught you all about that?"

Now I had him—he was back on familiar ground. But when I told him I wouldn't be coming home for a long time, it was more pain than he could conceal.

"Esau . . ."

"Don't let me catch you crying," I said, real soft.

Tory-boy fixed his gaze on me. One blink—dry eyes.

"You know how we watch TV together?"

"Sure!"

"We'll still do that. I'll be right next to you, like always. You won't see me, but I'll be there. I'll always be there, Tory-boy. If you talk to me, I'll answer. Right inside your head."

He nodded. But I wasn't sure he had it locked in as deep as I needed. So I said, "Didn't I swear to you that the Beast would never come into our place? Into any place we had?"

"Yes, Esau."

"It's been way over twenty years, Tory-boy. Isn't that long enough for you to believe me yet?"

"I always believe you!"

"Shhhh . . . I know you do. So you best believe me now when I tell you that I'll always be there, even if you can't reach out and touch me. I will never allow the Beast inside our place. Do you believe that?"

"Yes, Esau."

"That's my baby brother. My strong baby brother. That's what I've been waiting to hear. Now, tell me: are you still getting your checks?"

"Miz Avery brings me the money every month. The first Monday. She always does."

"Good. And what do you do with the money?"

"I keep one hundred dollars, and I give her the rest," he recited.

"Good! And she buys food and puts it in our house?"

"Yes, Esau. Every time."

The electricity and cable are paid right out of my account. Same for the propane. There's no landline, but the bank is set up for the cell-phone deductions, too. Tory-boy and me, we each have one. I've got all the right numbers programmed into his phone, and all the speed-dial numbers programmed into his head.

The Sheriff was letting me keep my cell phone in the jail, but I know they won't do that once I get to the penitentiary. Not unless money works as well in there as some people say it does.

But I'm playing it safe. I'll get Tory-boy ready for when he won't be able to call me anytime he wants. And there's enough in my bank account to cover my baby brother's bills for the rest of his life. Even if he lives to be a hundred, he'll never have to leave our place. Our safe place.

"You know who to take your car to?" I asked him. I deliberately said "your car," because, the quicker he got used to not using that van we had all fixed up for me, the better.

"Delbert's place. Every month."

"Perfect!"

He smiled when I praised him. If you want to see "innocent" for real, all you need is to watch Tory-boy smile. He doesn't have any badness in him. None. Tory-boy's as close to goodness as any man born of woman could ever be.

Delbert knew he had to keep our near-new Camaro factory-fresh. He got three hundred dollars a month for that, regular as clockwork, even if he didn't do anything but put gas in it.

"That car's still under warranty, Delbert. And I know Tory-boy's not going to be using up that kind of money on gas and oil changes," I'd told him when he came to visit me. "You're getting money. Regular. In cash. So there'll be plenty of extra for you to keep on the side. Sooner or later, that car's going to need work. I don't care if it needs a new engine, or transmission, or . . . anything. You have to keep *that* car working. That's the car Tory-boy knows. It has to last him his whole life, even if you have to replace every panel on the body and every bolt in the chassis. Fair deal?"

We shook hands.

There was no need for threats. I knew Delbert wouldn't cheat Tory-boy.

The man Tory-boy knew could never come inside our place had been a huge, powerful monster. I never used his name. I never called him "Dad," or "Father," or anything like that. It wasn't until Mrs. Slater snuck me over to church a few times while he was doing ninety days in the same jail they first put me in that I learned his true name. After that, in my mind, he was always "the Beast."

I don't know what names other people had for him, but I suspect they were similar. He was a man who'd stomp you or stab you just for getting in his way. The Beast really liked hurting people, and he didn't miss many opportunities.

Drunk, he was dangerous. Sober, he was lethal. If you crossed him, he'd kill you right where you stood . . . unless there were witnesses around.

Then he'd wait. And he wouldn't touch a drop until he settled up. When he was doing that kind of waiting, the Beast would go as quiet as a snake watching a rat.

In his own way, the Beast was a reliable man. If you did something to him, you could count on him coming for you.

But you'd never know when he was going to make his move. When it came to business, the Beast could bury his own ego in a cake of ice. He was proud of saying that an ambush is better than a gunfight.

Everybody hated him, but the Beast was always safe, because he had his place in the world. People needed him. Sometimes for certain kinds of work. But mostly what they needed was for him to leave them be.

Nobody needed for him to leave *us* be.

People don't take care of you just because it's the right thing to do. The law might prohibit some things, but a man owns his children same way he owns his livestock. Despite what some said, I never could find anything in the Bible to back that up, but there was no need—the Beast himself had taught me even before I could read.

He didn't teach me by talking; he showed me.

"Nobody's coming," he'd always say. "Nobody's ever coming here, you crippled little piece of shit. Not without my say-so. Not unless they want to die. It's my land they'd be stepping on. Ain't nobody around would do that, not even the Law."

The Beast knew people would always deal with you if you had something they wanted. He didn't have a friend in the world, but certain people always had work for him. "Jobs" is what he called that kind of work.

That's how I first learned that being safe is all about your place in this world—nothing else matters.

Later on, even when I was still a child, I could have found a place for myself alone easy enough. But had I done that, Tory-boy wouldn't've lasted out the week.

When Rory-Anne got big in the belly, I told the teachers I wouldn't be coming to school for a while. I could see they weren't all that upset, but they were obligated to ask me why that was.

When I told them Rory-Anne had a baby coming and I'd have to help her out, they just shook their heads.

Just like most people around here: they might get sad, but never enough to get helpful.

I read everything I could find about taking care of a baby, but there was no way around the one thing I'd never be able to do. If it wasn't for Mrs. Slater, Tory-boy never would have made it.

She came over one afternoon. The Beast's truck was gone, and a whole carful of people had come by and picked up Rory-Anne. I guessed Mrs. Slater had been watching, waiting for the right time.

"You know what every baby needs, son?" she asked me.

"Yes, ma'am. Milk."

"Is that what you've been crying over?"

"I guess so," I said, even though I didn't think there were any tears on my face—I had wiped it with my shirt soon as I heard the knock on the door.

"All right," Mrs. Slater said. "This is what we're going to do. Can you make it over to the lightning tree by yourself?"

"Yes, ma'am!" I was sure I could do that, because I'd already done it, plenty of times. That tree had been struck by lightning a long time ago—before I was born—and everybody steered clear of it because it's supposed to be real bad luck to touch such a tree.

The way I figured it, I'd already had about all the bad luck there was, so the lightning tree never spooked me.

And everybody avoiding it made it a perfect place for me to hide whatever I didn't want to keep in the shack.

Now that I think back on it, I'm sure Mrs. Slater had seen me go back and forth between that tree and our shack. She lived not a hundred yards from us, but way higher on the hill, in a much nicer house.

"God bless you," I said to her. I had nothing else to offer, and I was still young enough to believe that truly meaning what I said would count for something.

kept reading up on the subject, but mostly I learned just by taking care of the baby.

That was my job. Nobody had to say it; I just knew. I knew nobody else was going to do it if I didn't. I was bound to do it when I learned that Rory-Anne was going to give birth. But the first time I saw Tory-boy for myself, I *wanted* to do it.

This is the best way to make you understand that feeling I had: I wanted to protect him even more than I wanted to walk.

The wheelchair didn't stop me. I could roll right over, pick up Tory-boy, and do everything that had to be done. Just like I could pick up the milk Mrs. Slater left for me every day. It was always in actual baby bottles, in a little cooler. I knew how to heat it up, how to test it, and everything.

There was other stuff Mrs. Slater left, too. Mostly little jars of baby food, but there was also a blue blanket, stuff to put on Tory-boy's gums when his teeth were coming in . . . so many things I couldn't even count.

It was like Mrs. Slater had read the same books I had, because, every time a book said a baby would need something, she'd have it waiting for me.

When I was taking care of the baby, I knew he always had to be in the center of this gyroscope I was building in my mind. Maybe "gyroscope" isn't the right word: what I saw was all those spinning rings, constantly in motion around a center post. I don't know how I knew—it wasn't anything I'd read.

Maybe it was the spirits talking to me. That's the only way to explain how I was so dead certain about "balance" and "safe" having the same meaning.

I knew the exact nature of my balance. I could see it in my mind: swirling rings of pure black obsidian, every blade sharpened to such an edge that it made a surgeon's scalpel look like a flat rock.

Like everything of value, that perfect sharpness came at a price. Those "black knives" you can read about in Aztec legends were made from volcanic glass. Such a blade could be used only to slice, never to stab.

Somehow, I knew if I could always keep those rings spinning the center post would never fall over. It might lean—sometimes so far over that I'd be afraid—but it would not fall. No matter what hit against those rings, the center would stay upright.

I knew something else. I knew that, once anyone tried to cross into our side of those rings, me and Tory-boy would be safe from them, no matter what evil might be on their mind to do.

It may have been the only thing a half-person like me could ever manage to put together by himself—I had to do all the work inside my mind. But I knew, I absolutely knew, that if I used the half of me that worked I could get it done.

I never questioned how I knew this.

couldn't walk, but I could always get around. And I was so smart the teachers didn't know what to do with me. None of that made me safe. The Beast could unbalance my whole world just by tipping over my wheelchair.

He did that a lot, especially when he was drunk. Which was most of the time. But he did it when he was sober, too. He liked doing things like that. Liked showing you who was holding the whip hand. His favorite thing in life was raising fear in others.

Tory-boy might have been slow in the head, but he was fast on his feet. Soon as he could crawl, he would always try to scramble away when he heard the Beast coming. But there was no place to hide inside that miserable little shack, and he got hit on plenty.

Whenever the Beast went into one of his rages, Tory-boy would run to me. He never ran to Rory-Anne. He learned real quick that she wouldn't do anything. But even though I was only a child, and crippled to boot, Tory-boy developed the belief that I could protect him.

Maybe that was because, lots of times, I actually did. I knew that all I had to do was say the right words to the Beast and he'd forget about beating on Tory-boy and go right after me.

And I knew he'd stop a lot quicker if I didn't cry or scream. When he whipped Rory-Anne, the more she'd scream the longer he'd keep at it.

I think that's when I stopped feeling the hurt he put on me. After a while, I could see him doing it but it was like I was hovering above it all.

Every time he was finished with me, I would go find Tory-boy.

I'd cuddle him on my lap, rub his chest, and whisper soft until he stopped being afraid.

Years before he could understand words, I promised him that, one day, I'd make it stop. All of it.

For good and forever, I'd make it stop.

I chanted it like I was calling up a spell.

I didn't try praying. I had already figured out that God wasn't listening.

But once my little brother came, if I could have sold my soul to the Devil to make things right, I would have done it on the spot. And spit in the face of Jesus to seal the bargain.

Tory-boy believed anything I told him. He always did. And that was only right, because I never once lied to him.

Tory-boy had faith in me. True faith. I knew even the truest faith couldn't save people. They'd scream out in church how they'd been saved, but their lives would stay the same misery they'd always been. Nothing would change, yet their faith would persist. Like the people who tore up their lottery tickets and walked away chanting, "Maybe next time."

I'd had faith, once. The Bible was right about the Beast; I knew that was the truth even before I could read. So maybe God just didn't think me and Tory-boy were worth saving. But if He created us, how could that be? Why bother to plant rocks?

That was a puzzle I couldn't solve, so I put my trust where it belonged. Once I accepted Tory-boy's pure faith in me, it was up to me. Me, alone. My balance wasn't enough, not then. Even though I was building it, working on it constantly, I knew it would take time for me to get it perfect.

I didn't have that time. The only person I knew whose world was in balance was the Beast himself. I couldn't hope to match his balance. Only if I could find a way to disrupt it would he be vulnerable. Only then.

I watched him like he was under a microscope. I not only had to recognize the opportunity to disrupt his balance, I knew I'd only get the one chance to try it. If I failed, I wouldn't get a second one. The Beast would take me outside, crush my skull with a rock, and tell the Law I must've fallen out of my wheelchair.

It wasn't that I would have minded dying so much. But then Tory-boy would be left without protection. Not from the Beast, not from Rory-Anne, not from anyone at all.

I could not chance that. My plan had to be perfect. It had to throw the Beast's balance off so bad that he'd never get it back.

Somehow, I knew that that could be done, and that I could be the one to do it. I was always searching for a soft spot. I was . . . Ah, there's no truth in nice words. I needed to kill him. But I couldn't see how to do that, no matter how hard I looked.

It's a good thing I never needed much sleep—the only dreams I ever had were worse than being awake.

I kept studying. After a while, I learned about certain things that would poison a man to death. Plants I could find for myself, right out in the woods. Only, I also learned that it would take a long time—not hours, not days, weeks—for that kind of poison to work. I could cook, but it wasn't like the Beast was around to be fed every day.

It would only take a few seconds to blind him. I knew what I'd have to mix together to do that, and the Beast slept deep when he was drunk. But it was still too risky—even the smell of my fear might wake him up in time.

And, inside that shack, the Beast could find me and Tory-boy even if he was stone-blind—he'd done that in pitch-tar-black nights often enough.

I daydreamed about getting a pistol. I knew just the place to keep one hid. But I'd never used one, and I'd never get to practice shooting without drawing attention.

By then, I had one thing truly my own. My faith. Not the faith that makes you believe in things you'll never see, the faith you have in yourself.

By then, I knew all I needed was patience.

And I surely knew I had that by the ton. Patience may be a virtue, but I didn't need to be virtuous. I had such patience not because I was blessed with it, but because I learned it. When you're born under a curse, you *better* learn it.

Miss Webb was almost enough to make me believe there were angels on earth. She was the library lady, just out of the community college, not even twenty years old. Probably the only woman the County Library could find for the money it could pay.

It wasn't much of a library, and it was a few miles from where we lived, too. At first, I couldn't get over there but every once in a while. Then the school-bus driver started dropping me off at the library in the morning instead of taking me the rest of the way to school.

I realized that couldn't have been good luck—I knew there was no such thing, not for someone like me. And, sure enough, I found out later that Miss Webb had talked to him. There wasn't any point sending me to school when I was way smarter than the teachers. Besides that, some of the kids at school were as cruel as torture itself, and I couldn't waste any of my mind-time on fixing them—I had to devote every second to coming up with a way to kill the Beast.

I'd read and study at the library every day. All the books I ever asked for were science books—could be anything from physics to botany. Miss Webb never could have guessed what I was trying the hardest to learn from all that work.

The bus driver would pick me up in the afternoon and take me to where we lived. I think he must have been sweet on Miss Webb. It was for damn sure that nobody was paying him to carry me and my chair all the way to the door, both ways, like he did all during the week.

I wished I had a way to show my appreciation for that, besides just thanking him each time—that was nothing but common politeness.

I think the driver maybe even knew that. Because, when I asked him if I could know his whole name, he just said, "Charles Trammel, son. I mostly go by 'Charley,' but that there's my proper Christian name." I don't think he would have said all that if he couldn't tell that I felt bound to repay his kindness in some way.

Everybody at the school knew all about me spending my days at the library. But nobody ever said a thing about it. Who would they tell?

Miss Webb was the first girl I ever gave a Valentine card to. The only one ever, to be truthful about it.

She knew I could never bring books home—the Beast would tear them up just to be doing it. But I could bring the things she baked, and the big bottle of milk she always had for me, too, as long as me and Tory-boy could make them disappear quick enough. We got real good at that.

Miss Webb never tried to get me to read anything special; she just left me on my own. But she could get books I wanted just by ordering them from bigger libraries. I loved her for doing that even more than I loved her for feeding me and Tory-boy the way she did.

You are what you do. So I was able to love Miss Webb just for being herself.

I was a little ashamed of that feeling. I know I should have been wishing that Mr. Trammel and Miss Webb would get married, but I just couldn't make myself do that.

I'm not even going to lie and say I tried.

've had this sense of balance inside me ever since I can remember, but I didn't really feel it kick in until I found science. It was like a holy spirit, the way it beckoned me.

Preachers will say they "got the call." I don't know how it was for them—or even if they're being truthful when they make that claim. But for me, there could be no doubt. Science called: loud, hard, and sharp. A bright-white light calling, "You come this way, boy!"

Igniting something that had been inside me all the time, as congenital as my disease.

That does happen; I know it for a fact. Homer LaRue is the finest fiddle player there is, even if you'll never hear him on the radio. Folks say he just picked up an old fiddle one day and made it sing. Every year, people would come back from Branson and swear they hadn't seen anything to compare to him. And Homer LaRue never had a lesson in his life.

Folks say the music was born in him, but he didn't know that himself until it called him. That was like it was for me with science.

When Miss Webb saw me with an algebra book, she asked me if she could help me with it. I was stuck for a minute, like I was being pulled two different ways. I wanted to say yes; I always loved having her close to me. But I wanted to show off for her even more.

When I demonstrated that I already knew how to do all the problems, she couldn't hide her surprise. "Oh, Esau, I never imagined—" Admitting that she had underestimated me caused her to blush. It was the most beautiful thing I'd ever seen.

I was only about twelve or thirteen when it happened, but I remember it like it was yesterday.

And I will treasure it forever.

Oh, how I wanted to see that blush again. But I couldn't surprise her twice. After that, no matter what outlandish claim I'd make about what I knew, I couldn't even get her to raise her eyebrows.

It wasn't just killing I studied. I had to know about why me and Tory-boy had been so cursed. And I finally found the explanation I prayed wouldn't be there when I looked.

Once I followed the trail down to its natural end, I found myself studying genetics. After that, it didn't take me long to work it out.

I don't remember my mother. No, that's wrong. That's just dishonest. What I mean to say is that I have no actual memory of the Beast's woman—the one he always told people had run off on him. I knew that she hadn't given birth to me.

I remember thinking how, if her first child hadn't turned out to be a girl, she might have lived long enough to have actually been my mother.

I couldn't think past that point without crying, so, after a few tries, I stopped. For good.

Yes, I wanted it more than anything on earth. And, yes, I worked at it every waking moment. But when that flower finally reached full bloom, it wasn't due to any plan of mine.

It just happened, as if its time had come.

If people could look at a videotape of what happened, they'd get sick. And if they liked what they were seeing, they'd *be* sick.

The way it started, I didn't have any feeling about it at all. It wasn't new; it was part of my life. But when the Beast turned vulnerable, it was like looking at a beautiful new butterfly, opening its glistening wings as it rested up for its first flight. One of those rare sights, one you knew wouldn't last but a few seconds.

And something you'd maybe never see again.

I say it just happened because it started the way it always did. Rory-Anne came in real late one night. The Beast was waiting. He said he could smell it on her, what she'd been doing. Rory-Anne was too messed up to notice his eyes had already turned red.

He made us watch. I was nearly fifteen then; Tory—the child she'd named after herself—he was turning seven. Old enough for school, but nobody ever thought of sending him. He'd watched the Beast hurt Rory-Anne plenty of times, just as I had. He didn't understand that this time was going to be different. At first, neither did I.

The Beast had done all kinds of things to Rory-Anne before. We were used to it; she was used to it. He always called it "God's punishment for whores." First he'd use his belt on her, and then . . .

That night, when he was finished with the belt, he made her get on her knees. I thought I knew what was coming next—I'd seen that particular punishment a lot of times, even more since Tory-boy had been born.

By then, I knew why the Beast wanted Rory-Anne to get pregnant again. He wanted a baby girl.

The Beast unzipped his pants, but when he pulled his thing out, it just hung there, limp.

Rory-Anne burst out laughing at him. She called him all kinds of dirty stuff. I thought he'd beat her some more for that, but he just zipped up his pants and walked away. I figured he was headed for one of the bottles he always kept in his room.

When he walked back in, Rory-Anne was sitting on the couch. But she wasn't crying, she was having a good time. Kept calling the Beast all kinds of foul names, pointing at him, laughing like a crazy person.

"Good thing you can't get that little thing up no more, old man. Nigger cock tastes a lot better than yours, anyway."

She didn't stop talking that kind of stuff until she saw the pistol in his hand.

The Beast walked up real close to her and shot her in the face. Pieces of her head flew off behind her.

He looked at what was left of Rory-Anne's face like he expected her to say something. Seconds passed. Then he put down the pistol, spun around, and walked over to the kitchen. He came back with the butcher knife in his hand.

When he started to pull Rory-Anne's body by the hair, I knew what he was going to do. And, sure enough, he told me what to tell the cops if they ever showed up.

"I don't expect no cops," he told me. "That whore must've run off with someone. Not the first time she did that. But if they do show up . . ."

The Beast told me that if I didn't say what I was supposed to, say it exactly the way I was supposed to, the Law would carry him off.

"Then you wouldn't have nobody to take care of you and that little dummy," he said. When he saw that wasn't much of a threat, he told me if they put him in prison the Welfare would come and take me and Tory-boy away.

That didn't scare me, either. But the Beast knew me better than I thought. When he said the Welfare wouldn't just take me and Tory-boy away from the house, they'd take Tory-boy away from me, those words stabbed me right in my heart.

"They take me down for this and he's gonna be put in one of those schools for retards, you understand that? You know what those places are like? You seen those things I always done to that whore for punishment? That's what they'll do to him. They'll fuck him in his ass until he can't walk. Every day. Every night. But you won't get to see that for yourself. No, they'll put you in a place for crips. You'll never see that soft-in-the-head little freak again."

Maybe the Beast had never read a book, but he knew a lot. He was always sly—crafty in his ways.

It wasn't just that he knew telling me what was going to happen to Tory-boy would fill me with terror; he also knew the cops wouldn't believe any story he could make up. He knew most people believed he'd killed Rory-Anne's mother.

And why he'd done that, too.

Where we lived wasn't like what you see on TV—nobody was going to be digging up the ground looking for her body. But the Beast knew the cops wouldn't hesitate to take him away if he didn't have time to make Rory-Anne disappear. And if he had a pistol in his hand when they showed, they'd cut him down where he stood.

The Beast was a very crafty man. He knew I'd expect the Law to take me and Tory-boy away—with Rory-Anne dead, they'd have no choice. But he also knew the cops would believe anything I told them.

Everyone seemed to feel sorry for me, but kind of proud of me at the same time. They'd say what a shame it was, that spine thing, me being such a genius and all. After I won the State Science Fair, they said things like that even more.

Why would a boy like me tell a lie?

As the Beast talked, I felt the balance-power grow inside me. It became so powerful that it took over my entire spirit. I could feel it telling me that, for the first time in my life, I could put my own hand on the scales.

That feeling, it transformed me. Even my voice came out different. When I spoke to the Beast, he listened real close. It was like I was the one in charge, and he wanted to be sure he did everything I told him correctly.

What I told him was to give me his pistol, so I could put Rory-Anne's prints on it, too.

He looked at me strange when I said that, but he didn't argue. When I told him that nobody would believe any story about Rory-Anne running off, not with what they already suspected about his wife, he listened like missing a single word could cost him his life.

I told him how hard the ground would be that time of year; how it was already near four in the morning—it would be getting light too soon. If he tried to dig deep enough to bury Rory-Anne all by himself, he'd probably be caught in the act.

"The only way out for you is self-defense," I told him. "Now, you listen. I'm going to tell you what happened here, and I need you to memorize it."

He nodded his head when I spoke. If he'd been a dog, it would have signaled that he was submitting.

"That pistol there?" I told him. "That was Rory-Anne's. Not yours—hers. Understand? She always carried it around. I saw her put it in her purse myself, plenty of times.

"Now, what happened was, she just walked in the door, sat down on the floor, pulled out that pistol, and said she was going to kill herself.

"Rory-Anne said things like that before, but this time she wasn't playing. We both saw her pull back the hammer and hold it right to her head. That's when you jumped up and snatched it away from her.

"Next, you went into the bathroom to find some of her pills. I kept trying to calm her down, but she wouldn't listen to anything I said.

"Then she kind of staggered up on her feet. Before you could stop her, she ran into the kitchen, grabbed that butcher knife, and charged right at me, screaming and slashing like in that old *Psycho* movie.

"You didn't have any choice—if you hadn't shot her, she would have hacked me to death.

"There's plenty of proof of that. Rory-Anne always hated me. She hurt me before—just look at the back of my hand; they've got hospital records on that—but she never actually tried to kill me before.

"Maybe it was the drugs or the liquor—you know the cops are going to find plenty of both in her body when they cut her open."

I could see the Beast nodding to himself, taking it all in. Tory-boy was wailing. When I whispered to the Beast that I'd take care of the baby, get him to say the right things, too, he believed me.

Why shouldn't he? He knew Tory-boy would do anything I told him to do.

That was the first time the Beast ever acknowledged me. "You're a good son, Esau. And you always did have the brains in the family."

With that, he acknowledged something else: this time, I was driving the car. He was just a passenger.

I told him to go brush his teeth, get that alcohol smell off, clean himself up. We still had plenty of time. There was no phone in the house, and the Beast would have to walk up the hill to get Mrs. Slater to call the police. This time of night, he'd be waking her up. Wouldn't do if he showed up looking like he was drunk, would it?

He went right off to do like I told him. But somebody must've heard the shot. It had to have been Mrs. Slater, although nobody ever said. The Beast was still in the bathroom when the Law showed.

The Beast heard them pull up. He ran right out of the bathroom, his face still all soapy. He was just in time to hear me tell the cops how he made Rory-Anne get on her knees, then shot her like he was putting down a sick dog.

I had Tory-boy on my lap, holding him while I talked to the police. He was sobbing, and I was rubbing his chest to make him stop, the way I always did. None of the cops asked him any questions.

All the time they were cuffing him up, the Beast kept staring at me. He never said a word, but I could feel his hate. A white-hot arrow lanced out of each eye, seeking my soul.

I used my balance on those arrows. I could feel it working that time, just as I had felt his hate so many times before. But I was losing strength. Somehow, I knew my only chance was to get him *inside* the rings. And, sure enough, the very instant I parted those rings the Beast charged on through—he wanted to get at me so bad nothing else mattered.

That's when he learned that even his evil power wouldn't work from inside my balance rings. Every new blast he threw only made the blades spin faster and faster, stabilizing the center post. I was getting stronger, but the Beast kept on coming—it was all he knew.

A black-widow spider can kill a man. But if the man has that spider inside a glass jar, all the spider can do is wait—it's not his choice to make, not anymore.

At first, the DA was real worried. In fact, he was terrified. People around here don't pay much attention to what goes on in the court. They're a lot more interested in close-to-home gossip, like whether it's true about the pastor's wife and that guy they send out when your satellite dish needs an adjustment. But get yourself known for losing a big trial—especially one people really wanted you to win—and they *will* remember that.

"No offense, son, but your sister did have herself quite a reputation, if you know what I mean."

I knew what he meant, all right. But it wasn't Rory-Anne's reputation that made the DA's hands tremble and his voice go thin; it was the Beast's.

The DA was standing between two men on a dueling ground. He knew if he offered a nice enough deal—say, two, three years in prison—the Beast would not only snatch at it, he'd be beholden to him as well. But then the town would have a new thing to gossip about.

And not the usual petty stuff—rumors of corruption would be flying about. Worse yet, everyone wanted the Beast gone, and they expected the DA to handle that business for them.

There was no real possibility of compromise. The DA was an expert in such things, but no matter how he tested those waters, they came up foul. So he not only had to charge the Beast with murder, he had to make it stick.

Sure, he was a politician, and he didn't want to chance losing an election. But this was worse. A whole lot worse. When you dealt with the Beast on any matter, win-or-lose always came down to live-or-die. Either he'd owe you a debt, or you'd owe him a death.

If the DA lost *any* murder trial, that would cost him some prestige. But if the Beast walked out of the courtroom without shackles on his wrists, the DA knew it was only a matter of time before dirt would be shoveled over his own coffin.

I t's not a question of believing you, Esau. I know you wouldn't lie. But juries are funny—you just never know how they're going to act."

"But—"

"Let me finish, now, son. It's not as cut-and-dried as you seem to think. See, we don't really have that 'forensics' stuff juries expect to see today. All that damn TV, it's polluted their minds. Sure, we have the pistol, we have the bullet, and we can prove that your father . . ."

I hadn't said anything, but he must have felt some of the rage coming off me when he used that word. The Beast wasn't my father. He wasn't anybody's father.

". . . that the defendant"—he switched words so smoothly that I knew he must have had a lot of practice—"shot the . . . victim. But there was that butcher knife out in plain view, and everyone in the house had left some prints on it. Even you.

"So what it comes down to is one person's word against another's. And that's never a choice you want to leave up to a jury."

"There isn't a person in this town that wouldn't take my word over his," I told him.

"I'm not saying that isn't true. But Lord knows your sister had good reason to hate that man. You, too, truth be told. And everybody in this town knows that, too."

When a silver-tongued man says something blunt, you'd best listen. The DA was warning me what was going to come out at the trial—what would be all the motivation I would ever have needed to hate the Beast. Even enough to lie under oath.

I visualized a horde of savage termites attacking our house, boring their way in so deep that the wood was going to collapse in on itself.

I reached desperately for my balance like a man grabbing for a handhold while tumbling down a quarry wall. I clawed my hands until they caught. Then I hauled myself up, hand over hand. A man doesn't need legs for that.

That's when I started talking. And I didn't stop until I'd blocked those termites with my sworn promise that the DA would never lose that trial.

I promised him that by the time they held that trial Tory-boy would be a witness, too. Nobody would doubt anything a child like Tory-boy said—they'd know he couldn't make up a lie if he wanted to.

I even told the DA he could test it for himself. Give me a couple of months to work with my baby brother. Then he could ask Tory-boy anything he wanted. If he didn't like the answers, he could make whatever deal with the Beast he wanted to.

The DA, he was an important man. Not just a lawyer, the prosecutor over the whole county. But when I looked into his eyes, I saw just what I expected to see.

I think maybe that was the first time I realized the full truth about how having your place in the world was the only thing that could keep you safe.

For as long as people needed you, you were safe from them.

For that long, and no longer.

The DA had Tory-boy tested. They let me be there while they did it—they knew they couldn't leave him in a room with a bunch of strangers and expect much more out of him than throwing a fit. And even at his age, nobody wanted to be around Tory-boy when he went off.

The social workers and the psychologists wrote reports. They all said the same thing. They sometimes used different terms, but "developmentally delayed" was their clear favorite.

That just means slow, not stupid. No reason in the world why Tory-boy couldn't do the same things other children did, he'd just always be a little behind his years, and he'd never catch up.

Although he tested out to have a mental age of about five, Tory-boy was almost nine at the time. So first they had to hold this little trial—I think they called it a "hearing" because there was no jury there—to see if he'd be allowed to testify at all.

The judge was real clear about that—it wasn't the age of the witness that mattered; it was whether he knew the difference between telling the truth and telling a lie. And whether he knew it was wrong to tell a lie.

Some children were so young that, no matter how smart they might turn out to be later in life, they couldn't do those things. A two-year-old, you wouldn't expect he could do that.

But a five-year-old, he could. So, even if Tory-boy was behind other kids his own age, he might be allowed to testify. That's what we were all there to find out.

The Beast's lawyers only had a couple of hours to break Tory-boy. They'd've had a better chance of digging a mine shaft with their bare hands.

Two hours, when I'd had every other hour of his life to teach him what he needed to know. Passing school tests wasn't my concern; I just had to teach my little brother how to answer the kind of questions that I knew were going to be asked. The DA gave me some transcripts to study first, so it was even easier.

It wasn't about memorizing. I had Tory-boy's total, absolute trust. If I told him he had seen something happen, he *had* seen something happen.

He looked so magnificent in court, sitting up straight, handsome and proud. What he was proud of was that he knew the answers I'd taught him—I was the only person in the world he'd ever wanted to please.

"A lie is when you say something that isn't true," he spoke right up, clear and confident.

One of the Beast's lawyers—the older one—tried to trip up Tory-boy by asking a long, complicated question. But Tory-boy was ready for him. He remembered what I'd taught him to say, and he'd die before any old man in a suit could make him say different.

"Well, then," the Beast's lawyer asked, "how do you know when something isn't true?"

"A truth is what is real. If something really happened, and you say what really happened, you're telling the truth."

The lawyer kept trying, but you could see Tory-boy had taken all the heart out of him. Finally, the judge stepped in and took over.

"Do you know the difference between a truth and a lie, son?" he asked Tory-boy.

"A truth is right. A lie is wrong."

"What happens if you tell a lie?"

"Telling a lie is a sin," Tory-boy recited, letter-perfect. "If you tell lies, you burn in Hell."

"Seems clear enough to me, counsel," the judge said to the Beast's lawyer. "There's plenty twice his age who don't know as much as this boy does."

"But, Your Honor—"

"Enough!" the judge snapped at him. "You're asking the same questions over and over. We are finished with this witness." I took that as a signal to roll over to where Tory-boy had been sitting and pick him up. I was almost eighteen then, but Tory-boy was damn near my size. If it wasn't for all those years rolling myself around, all those exercises I did with Tory-boy, I doubt I could have carried him away like I did.

We sat right next to each other in the back of the courtroom, just waiting to see what would happen next.

"I'll hear oral argument," the judge said.

"With all respect, this is *res ipsa,* Your Honor," the DA said. "The standard has not only been met, it's been satisfied with room to spare."

"The only *'res ipsa'* here is that the boy is retarded," the Beast's lawyer fired back. "There's no dispute about that. In the *Morrison* case, this state's highest court held that—"

"This court is quite familiar with *Morrison,*" the judge said. You could tell he was insulted, like this outsider was questioning if he was retarded himself. "As you undoubtedly know, counsel, *Morrison* referred to a child found to be so profoundly retarded that he was unable to do anything more than babble a few simple words, with no regard to their actual meaning.

"Furthermore, *Morrison* was a civil case, concerning charges of sexual abuse brought against the owner and several employees of a private care facility. The matter before this court is distinguishable on several grounds."

"I certainly was not implying—"

"Sir," the judge said, using that word without a drop of respect in it, "this court has made a finding. I trust you are familiar with your appellate remedies. If you believe you can get past the threshold of outright frivolousness, I assume you will act accordingly."

When the judge cracked his gavel down, you could see where he wished he could have cracked it.

We waited until everyone had filed out of the room. As the DA passed me, he moved his head just enough to let me know that, next time I told him I could make something happen, he wouldn't doubt me, not ever.

Not ever *again,* is what he meant.

The trial itself came almost a year after that hearing, so I had plenty of time to teach Tory-boy some new things. The DA told me what questions the Beast's attorneys would be likely to ask, and I worked my little brother until he had it down perfect.

"Most capital cases try for delay," the DA told me. "*This* delay is going to help the defendant right into the Death House."

You don't get a performance like that from a child out of fear. Just the opposite, in fact. If Tory-boy hadn't wanted to please me more than anything in the world, he could never have managed the task.

Lord, how his face would light up every time I told him what a fine boy he was!

When the State called Tory-boy as a witness, they let me wheel him up to the stand. I couldn't stay there with him, but they let me move my chair over to one side, so Tory-boy would know I was still there.

The Beast's lawyer raised all kinds of holy hell about that. He said I was going to be a witness, too, so I shouldn't be allowed to stay anywhere in the courtroom at all.

But the judge was ready for that. He read off a whole long string of different cases where what he called a "vulnerable witness" was allowed to testify under special conditions. The one I remember most was when they let a little girl who'd been raped by her stepfather take the stand with a dog sitting right next to her. The dog was trained to be with kids when they testified; she helped them be calm when they had to talk about terrible things that had happened to them.

The lawyer for the Beast still wasn't satisfied. He switched gears, said I could be giving Tory-boy the answers, signaling to him in some way.

"Let me understand, counsel," the judge said. "Are you saying that a child whose testimony you sought to bar on the ground that he was mentally incapable of distinguishing the truth from a lie has now acquired the power to translate some secret signals from his brother into answers to questions you ask him under oath?"

"No, Judge. I'm not saying that. But, still, even the appearance of impropriety—"

"There *is* no such appearance," the judge chopped off whatever the lawyer was going to say. "Unless you can show this court that the witness is some kind of ventriloquist's dummy in the hands of his caregiver, your motion is denied."

The DA jumped to his feet. "Your Honor, may the record reflect that, regardless of any ludicrous claims by defense counsel, the matter is moot, as the witness's caregiver is sitting well beyond the sight line of the witness?"

"So ordered," the judge said.

I'd never heard myself called a "caregiver" before, but, from the way the judge had leaned so heavy on that word, I knew it had to have some special legal meaning. I even forgave him for using the word "dummy."

All the DA did was to stand close to Tory-boy, making sure the jury could see he wasn't coaching, just treating a child the way you're supposed to. He didn't have but one question:

"Can you tell us what happened that night, son?"

And Tory-boy spoke right up: "Mommy was on the couch. Daddy made her get down. Then he took his gun and shot her. In the face. Bang!"

The Beast's older lawyer was some geezer the County had paid for; the Beast himself didn't have any money, so they had to do that. Even so, that lawyer really tried, but he couldn't move my little brother an inch. Once Tory-boy had something in his head, it stayed there. Unless I moved it out. I was the only one who could ever do that.

"No, no, no," Tory-boy kept saying. Over and over again. Then he started crying a little, because the lawyer was being mean to him, and he knew it.

Everyone in the courtroom knew it.

But every time the lawyer tried to stop asking Tory-boy any more questions, everyone saw the Beast raging at him to get back in there and try again.

The harder that lawyer tried to push Tory-boy, the more you could feel the anger against him vibrating through the courthouse. Especially from the women. What kind of lowlife would scream at a poor little retarded boy, making him cry and all?

That lawyer wasn't local—the county covers a lot more territory than the town where we lived—but he wasn't from that far away. When he felt those waves hit, even the Beast couldn't make him ask Tory-boy one more question.

When they put me on the stand, both of the Beast's lawyers had a turn, and they didn't have to hold back. But every question they asked me was giving me a chance to put another spike in the Beast's chest. And I hammered those spikes like I was John Henry himself.

"You hate this man, don't you?" the younger lawyer shouted at me, pointing to where the Beast was sitting.

"You mean for beating us all the time? I may have hated him while he was doing that, especially to my little brother, sir. I admit that. I keep working on forgiving him, and I believe I might be able to do that, someday. But I don't know if I can ever forgive him for killing my sister—"

"Objection!"

"Invited error, Your Honor," the DA shouted back.

"You opened the door, counsel," the judge told the Beast's lawyer, barely able to keep the smile off his face.

I was grateful the jury couldn't read my thoughts then. I didn't even know a half-man like me could have a battle cry, but I could hear it ring out inside my mind: *Yeah, you opened that door, Beast. And I just rolled right on through it, didn't I? Now what?*

I felt powerful enough to knock that lawyer out without ever leaving my chair, but I didn't let it show on my face. It didn't matter what that man said, it didn't matter what tricks he tried, the jury never took its eyes off me. And they all listened like I was sanctified.

Even with all that, the Beast still might have gotten off with only a few years. The DA about threw a fit over it, but the judge told the jury they could consider lesser charges. He read a whole list of them: manslaughter, involuntary homicide . . . even felonious assault, which sounded like nothing more serious than a slap on the face.

If the Beast had admitted he'd just plain shot Rory-Anne, it might have come out differently. If he'd said he was so drunk he hardly remembered that whole night, the jury might well have believed him.

It's not that anyone liked him, but, in their eyes, there would have been a lot of truth being told in any story the Beast could make up. The men knew what kind of temper he had, especially when he was drunk. And the women, well, they knew all about Rory-Anne.

The Beast knew I wasn't ever going to tell anyone about what he'd been doing to Rory-Anne for all those years. How could I? If he had told some sad story about how his wife had run off and left him to raise Rory-Anne all on his own, and she had just gone wild after that, he knew I wouldn't call him a liar.

He knew if I disputed his story it would be just the same as telling the whole town the truth about me and Tory-boy. Folks may have suspicioned, but I'd never allow them to turn that suspicion into truth out of my own mouth.

Maybe the Beast was scared they'd finally start looking for his wife's body. Or . . . Well, I'll never know why, but he got right up on the stand and insisted he was stone-cold sober the night it happened.

He *still* swore he'd just been trying to stop Rory-Anne from killing me with that butcher knife. He told the whole courtroom that all he'd done was try to protect his crippled son from that crazy, drunken whore.

But all the while he was telling that pack of lies, he never stopped glaring at me. The whole courtroom could see those vile threats flash, as if someone was striking his flinty eyes with a piece of steel.

The State always has to go first, so the Beast had already heard Tory-boy and me tell the jury a different account entirely. But he stayed stuck to his story, as if he couldn't get that seed I had planted out of his head.

Just like I could never get the seed he planted in Rory-Anne out of my body.

With Rory-Anne dead, I was in charge. Before, even though me and Tory-boy each got Disability checks, they came to her—that's how they do it with children. But Rory-Anne touched those checks just long enough to sign them over to the Beast.

Probably another reason he'd never killed us.

Or maybe he thought Rory-Anne would do it for him. She'd thrown knives at me more than once—it really drove her crazy whenever I would try to keep her off Tory-boy.

But even though the government considered me disabled, there wasn't a soul in town who thought there was anything wrong with my mind. So, with the Beast and Rory-Anne gone, both checks came to me directly.

Maybe they bent a law a little bit to do that; I'm not exactly sure. I know they made me what they call an "emancipated minor" before the Beast was even put on trial. But they didn't stop there; they made me Tory-boy's legal guardian as well.

The judge said that was only right, seeing as I was the only family he had, what with my mother gone, my sister dead, and my father sure to be in prison for life . . . if he got lucky.

"The whole town knows you raised that child since he was born, Esau," he said. Talking to me direct, not even glancing at that "Rural Services" lawyer who was supposed to be helping me. She was an outsider. We didn't need any such people telling us how to take care of our own business.

"We're all proud of the job you've done. Tory's never been a bit of trouble to anyone. And, you know, some of those . . . slower ones, they can fall in with the wrong crowd. But this court is satisfied that if there's one person he minds it's you."

That was true. Nobody ever did deny that. Not even the Beast.

I knew the first thing we had to do was get some money. Magic be damned, that shack would always hold memories Tory-boy might not be able to deal with.

Getting money turned out to be easier than I thought. Once I started really concentrating on doing it, that is.

Every night, after Tory-boy fell asleep, I went back to science. Spina bifida isn't so rare as you might think. Not everyone who's born with it has to be in a wheelchair. It depends on what type you have.

Turns out, I had drawn the shortest straw. When the vertebrae don't form correctly, a little sac filled with fluid extends through an opening in the spine. That's called "myelomeningocele." It can hit just about anywhere along your spine, so I guess it was lucky for me that it happened at the lowest point—because anything below that point is never going to work the way it should.

If Rory-Anne hadn't been convinced they'd give her all kinds of drugs, I probably wouldn't have been born in a hospital. That's all that saved me. They even had to put a shunt in my head to drain the fluid buildup. I still have the scar from that, but that's the only sign I carry. Above the waist, I mean.

I know they'd told Rory-Anne I was what they call an "at-risk" baby, but she never once brought me back to the hospital until that time she burned me and got scared.

Every time I came across something that said aftercare was critical for babies born with spina bifida, I wondered why the County had never sent anyone around to check. But then I remembered the Beast. If those social workers wanted to come and have a look at me, they'd need to bring the cops with them. I guess it wasn't worth all that trouble. Not for someone like me, anyway.

So I grew up not being able to really use any part of my body from the end of my spine on down. I accepted that. Just like I accepted the jolts of pain that shot the length of my left leg all the way into my central nervous system.

I say "accepted," but that came slow. The first time, I was about nine years old, and that pain blast filled me with terror. I thought I was dying. Worse, I thought of what would happen to Tory-boy without me to protect him.

But then it stopped. *Snap!* Just like that. As if the very thought of Tory-boy being hurt drove the Devil of that pain right back down to Hell, where it belonged.

It wasn't until I started looking for ways to get more money for me and Tory-boy to be safe that I read about how some folks with the exact same disease I had could actually feel something below the waist, too.

That comforted me considerably. It confirmed what I knew in my own mind—what I had felt wasn't this "phantom pain" thing some of the books talked about. It was as real as the disease itself.

I was thankful for that knowledge. I understood how things were always going to be. I knew if I couldn't control my own mind, I'd never be able to control anything at all.

So my curse wasn't unique like I'd once thought—others had my exact same condition. I had kin I'd never meet. Brothers and sisters who were sort of semi-paralyzed but could still feel pain, same as me. Born bad, both ways. As if we'd all been at the same table, all rolled the dice together. And thrown snake eyes.

But I didn't want to "share" in some therapy group. I didn't need advice on learning to "cope." I had responsibilities. And now that I knew others with my condition could feel pain, I knew there was a way for me and Tory-boy both.

All I needed was the money to pay what it would cost.

Truth was, most of the time I hardly felt anything at all. And when that pain would spike, I'd just breathe real slow and think about how good a child Tory-boy was. I learned to drop so deep into that thought that when I opened my eyes the pain would be gone.

Dr. Harris never said a word when I kept telling him I needed more and more of those painkillers. All opiates are dose-related, so it was only natural that what blocked the pain would lose its power over time.

It wasn't any problem at all for me to get a permanent scrip for heavier and heavier hits of OxyContin, with another for morphine-by-injection, and then still another for the Fentanyl transdermals, for when the terrible pain in my withered legs got so unbearable that I had to have some medication going constantly.

Dr. Harris didn't even blink. No surprise there. That's what folks said about him—he hated pain like it was his personal enemy. That shouldn't be an unusual thing, but it is. There are plenty of doctors around here who're so scared of the DEA that they wouldn't give Vicodin to a man dying of bone cancer.

The pharmacist never raised an eyebrow at all the scrips I kept handing over. And if the Internet stores had any problem, they never told me about it.

The only pain all that stuff actually killed was the pain of poverty. The drugs brought in a steady supply of cash. People who wanted to get high could crush the OxyC into a powder and snort it, or pour it into a shot of whiskey. The Fentanyl could be boiled right out of the patches. And the morphine even came with its own supply of clean needles.

The way we worked it was like this: anyone who wanted drugs would leave the money in the mailbox at the end of our lane, then push the button inside the plastic box right underneath it. I built that box so the button would stay dry, no matter what the weather.

When I saw the light flash inside our place, I'd send Tory-boy to walk on down, pick up the cash, and bring it back to me.

I could always tell by the amount what was wanted, but some people left notes anyway. Whenever that happened, I'd tell Tory-boy to take it all back—the money and the note. The way I reasoned it, everybody knew my rates, so I treated any note like it was the Law, trying to trap me.

People knew I had to have a sizable amount of drugs on hand to fill those orders, but even with all the junkies we have around here, none of them even thought about ripping off my stash.

Dope fiends risk their lives every time they stick a needle in their veins or snort something up their noses. A risk, not a certainty—they're not the same thing. For all I know, risk is part of the jolt addicts are always chasing.

Trying to break into our place wouldn't be a risk; there was no doubt about the outcome.

Our three pit bulls are brothers from the same litter. We got them from Donna Belle Parsons, down at the shelter. Some piece of trash had thrown a pit bull bitch out the window of a moving car. They probably figured she was all bred out.

Their stupidity is what saved our dogs. That bitch was not only pregnant when they dumped her, she was tough enough to stay alive almost six more weeks. Once she delivered, she closed her eyes and went to sleep, her last fight finally over.

Donna Belle Parsons wouldn't have let most folks take more than one pup, especially those not even weaned. She harbored a deep, abiding hatred for dogfighters.

There's a number of bunchers in these parts. That's what they call men who go around grabbing dogs any way they can, so they can sell them to the dogfighters to use as training meat for their killers. Miss Parsons could smell a buncher at a hundred yards. If one came into her shelter, he was putting his life on the line.

That's not talk, that's fact. Donna Belle Parsons kept a pistol behind the counter. Tommy Joe Knowles still walks with a limp because he'd thought she wouldn't use it.

I've noticed that men make that mistake about women all the time. Donna Belle Parsons was a tall, shapely woman, with a real pretty face and a sweet, soft voice. But the only reason Tommy Joe walks with a limp is because she hadn't aimed that pistol of hers at his thick head.

'd shown Tory-boy how to hold the little bottle for the pups, and he got real good at it. Now they're almost three years old. And if anybody or anything except me or Tory-boy came near our shack, they'd rip it apart, tearing off pieces like I'd seen those sharks do on TV.

It might be another pit who got loose from one of the dog-fighters' pens, might be a cat who should have had more sense, might be a sheriff, might be a preacher—to our dogs, it wouldn't make any difference. Cross their line and you'd end up a shredded corpse.

They didn't act like that because they were mean—they were just doing their job. Tory-boy loved those dogs. He named them One, Two, and Three.

Tory-boy was always patting them and cuddling them like they were big toys. That was the original reason I wanted to get pit bulls: most people think they're just plain vicious, like it's in their blood. It's true enough that people have been breeding them since forever to be vicious, but that's vicious to other dogs, not to people.

You ever try and get near a dog that's been hit by a car? Even though all you want is to help that dog, he'll snap at you like a viper. Not a pit bull. If they were like that, how could people who fight them handle them down in the pit? How could they patch them up in the middle of a fight and send them right back to the scratch line?

Tory-boy didn't know how strong he was. So, when he started begging me for a puppy, I was afraid that he'd break one in half just petting it. That's why I got him pups that were real strong themselves. I'd seen other pit bulls around little kids. Watched the kids pull their tails, squeeze them hard enough to crack a rib, even poke them in the eye . . . but those dogs acted like they didn't even feel it.

Turns out, I needn't have bothered. Once I showed Tory-boy

how, he hand-raised those pups. We fed them the best food, made sure they had all their shots, sheepskin blankets to sleep on, rawhide to gnaw on. Everything they wanted in life, it was me and Tory-boy who gave it to them. They reasoned it out the way animals do—anybody who threatened us was threatening them.

Our dogs weren't the kind you want to threaten. A bully might be dangerous, but a protector is deadly.

We never locked our door. It was only plywood anyway. The dogs always let us know when anyone was near. Just a quiet little growling, deep in their throats, with the hair raised on the backs of their necks. Anytime they'd get like that, we'd all just sit and wait. Me, Tory-boy, and the dogs, all together in the dark.

But after a while, the dogs would lie down and make another little sound. A different one. Probably telling each other how disappointed they were.

It wasn't only drugs that kept money coming in. Tory-boy just got stronger and stronger. He could work like two mules, so there was always some extra cash anytime we might need it.

And before long, I was doing work for certain people. After that, it was just a matter of building our money until we had all we needed to make my plans come true. All my plans, even the exit one.

Not a day passed but that I didn't do some kind of work with Tory-boy, and he got pretty good at most things. As long as he didn't speak up, people usually just took him for quiet. And when he was wheeling me around to see different people, I would do all the talking. Not to disguise anything—to teach Tory-boy more about the kind of answers you give to certain questions.

And manners. I was known for my manners; everyone said what a gentleman I was. I wanted them to say the same about Tory-boy, and I know he copied me every way he could think of.

By the time he was fifteen, Tory-boy was such an outright ox that the high-school football coach paid us a visit. That was right after I won a hundred dollars from Jasper Murdle when Tory-boy lifted the back end of Jasper's old Chevy right off the ground like it was a box of cereal.

The coach told me not to worry about Tory-boy's grades, never mind his IQ—all that kind of thing could be taken care of. He told me what Tory's contribution to the team would mean to the whole town. I tried to stay polite, but the man made it more and more difficult.

He was so determined that I had to put in some real work to make him understand that there was no way to put Tory-boy out on a field with boys slamming into each other. Sooner or later, Tory-boy would cripple someone, or even kill them, and then the whole story would come out. Did the coach want to be the one to explain how a straight-A student couldn't read or write?

I was almost thirty-four when the State finally executed him. A lot of folks praised Jesus when they got the news. I may be no match for them in church attendance, but they were putting the credit where it didn't belong. I was the one who had truly slain the Beast.

I was so proud that day. With him gone, I thought I'd made Tory-boy safe forever.

We'd had our own house for some time by then. Not a trailer, a for-real house, with a nice porch, a fine roof, and plenty of room. There was even a special bathroom built for me.

Our house sat on more than ten acres of ground, too. Most of it wasn't cleared, and there wasn't any fence around it that you could see. But anybody who stumbled across the first electrical barrier would see the flashing red lights and get their message.

That message spread. It got so we wouldn't see that flash for months at a time.

Not many folks around here pay cash for a house, but they all gossip. I didn't want extra attention, so I took out a mortgage, 10 percent down. Those payments came right out of the bank account, too, along with the property taxes and the insurance. Hardly made a dent.

We didn't need the "our place" spell anymore. Tory-boy always felt safe now. The Beast would never come back, never torment him again.

They'd taken him away for killing Rory-Anne. The "guilty" verdict, that was expected. But it was the Beast's own testimony that had brought it all the way up to Murder One.

When that happens, they hold another trial to decide what happens to the defendant. That's how I knew all about that "penalty phase" thing before I ever faced it myself, so many years later.

Once it was a sure thing that the Beast was going to be caged for a long time—the lightest Murder One sentence here is life without parole—it seemed like half the people in town had some story to tell about him.

If ever a man needed killing, it was him. They all said that, one way or another. A few actually said those very words.

Of course, none of those cowards had ever said so out loud before that day.

It was the first time anyone could remember that Pastor Booker didn't testify in such a case. You could always count on him to talk about how some killer found Jesus while he was awaiting his sentence. He'd always say every man was worthy of a chance to redeem himself, even behind bars.

Pastor Booker not speaking up for the Beast, that was the same as him saying he'd finally found a man who was past even God's forgiveness.

The Beast had the right to put on his own witnesses, too. That was as valuable to him as the right to drink a glass of cyanide.

The jury stayed out just long enough to make it look as if they'd actually considered the matter. When they came back, they carried the death penalty along with them.

The Beast lasted a long time before they finally put him down. I remember the first appeal. The DA called me and told me about it—some kind of challenge to Tory-boy's testimony, claiming he wasn't competent to testify.

When the DA asked me to come down to his office a few months later, it was only so he could crow in front of an audience. He showed me where the appeals court wrote that the "thorough and objective questioning of the child by the trial judge" prior to allowing Tory-boy to testify was sufficient. More than sufficient.

They made that last part real clear. I didn't have to be a lawyer to understand what they meant by the "overwhelming weight of the evidence." Even if Tory-boy had never said a word, there were enough reasons to find the Beast guilty a dozen times over. And not a single one to spare his life.

I had stopped worrying about the Beast a long time ago. I knew he was already dying, no matter how any of his appeals might turn out. They'd already taken him off the Row and moved him to the prison hospital.

The way I heard it, there was this cat that had the run of the Row. He didn't belong to any particular prisoner, but most of them saved up treats for him, made toys for him to play with, patted him every chance they got. Always proving to that cat that they were worthy of being his friend.

Somehow, the Beast lured the cat to come into his cell. A few minutes later, he threw the cat's dead body out through the bars, its head twisted so bad it had about come off.

None of that was in the newspapers, but it came to me from a very reliable source.

A few weeks after that happened, the Beast started screaming in the middle of the night. The guards let him carry on for a few hours, until morning, when the prison doctor made his regular rounds.

The doctor couldn't find anything, so they took him over to the clinic for X-rays. Still nothing, so they threw him back in his cell.

But the Beast kept running a real high fever. Even the pain-killers couldn't calm him down. After a while, he couldn't even take food; they had to keep him alive with an IV tube.

Finally, they took him to an outside hospital, under heavy guard. They knocked him out and opened him up, but what they called "exploratory surgery" came up with more questions than answers.

It was all very mysterious. The Beast's whole intestinal tract was lacerated—"as if the patient had swallowed finely ground glass," one report said—and he also had certain symptoms of septic shock you could only get from being poisoned. But the Beast had eaten exactly the same meal as everyone else on the Row the night he took sick.

No responsible party was ever identified.

I know all that last part because the Beast's lawyers had made an application for a pardon, on compassionate grounds. They said he was barely alive, in constant pain, too weak to be a danger to anyone.

The DA showed me a copy of the pardon application. This time he wasn't boasting; he wanted my opinion, he said. I knew what he really wanted without him having to say a word. He needed me to write out that me and Tory-boy were still terrified of the Beast.

I could do that, easy enough. But, seeing as I was there anyway, I asked the DA if he believed the Beast was too weak to pull a trigger.

He liked that so much he put it into the thick stack of papers he filed against letting the Beast out on any grounds. The State put him in the Death House to die—die healthy, die sick, made no difference in the eyes of the law.

But the Beast's lawyers kept on trying, right up to the night the prison changed what they'd been sending down that IV tube.

When he was just a child, some of the kids would do cruel things to Tory-boy. Not just torment him; some of what they did was downright evil, done for its own sake. Most of the time, I would wheel myself over and talk to the other kids' folks, usually their mothers.

By the time I arrived, anyone could see how much effort I'd had to put in to make the trip. And I was always polite and respectful when asking their help.

I made sure they understood I knew I couldn't take the chance of telling the Beast. Not that anyone thought he cared about his children—he just never needed much of an excuse to hurt people, and *that* they knew real well.

Most of the time, the kid who'd been doing things to Tory-boy, he'd get a whipping, and the promise of more to come if he ever did it again. Decent people don't hold with picking on a little boy who isn't right in his head.

After the Beast first got sent away, I didn't have the implied threat of his violence going for me. Still, I was usually successful. But not every time. So I had to learn how to fix such things myself.

That turned out to be not so difficult as you might imagine. Folks around here put a lot of stock in signs. Omens. "Portents" is what the elders called them.

So, when things kept happening to the parents of kids who tormented Tory-boy, people started talking.

There was plenty for them to talk about. It was no secret that I loved my little brother. That much was fact. God knows Esau Till has got him one powerful mind, people would say. But maybe he had other powers, too: casting spells, hexing, putting the evil eye on someone.

I know what Mrs. Birdsong said about me. She's over one hundred years old, folks say. That's a woman you listen to when she speaks. The way it was told to me, what she said was:

"Satan cursed that poor boy, crippling him so bad like he is. And that wasn't the only cross Esau has had to bear. But he never turned his back on the Lord. Nobody ever knew him to feel sorry for himself, or ask for pity. And look how he raised that brother of his all by himself. That's a *good* man there. God and Satan, they're always at war. God can't undo Satan's work, but He can grant the strength to overcome it, if you're worthy. So it could be that God Himself blessed Esau with powers. Everyone knows how smart that boy is. You think that's an accident? Maybe he's even smart enough to use some of Satan's own spells on those who do him wrong."

I remember one of those parents that something truly terrible happened to. He was a short, stocky man with big arms and cruel eyes. When I told him his two sons had made Tory-boy eat dirt in front of everyone, he said if that big-head little brother of mine couldn't take care of himself, that wasn't his problem—nobody was going to tell him how to raise his own kids. "That father of yours ain't around no more, crip. So just wheel yourself on out of here."

When they found that man, his face was split all the way through. That can happen when the brake on your chainsaw fails—it can kick right back on you, still spinning all those killer steel teeth.

People just shook their heads. Had to happen sooner or later, they said. Everyone knew that man was an idiot with machinery. Probably been drinking, too.

After a while, nobody tried to tell Tory-boy to eat dirt anymore. Maybe some did believe I had hexing power. But what stopped them dead in their tracks was that Tory-boy's strength was just enormous. Nobody knew its limits, and that was something they damn sure didn't want to find out for themselves.

Later on, instead of tormenting Tory-boy, different people would ask him about going along on some kind of crime with them. And he'd always say the same thing: "I got to ask my brother."

Anyone with a drop of sense would leave it at that. But, one time, some fool just had to say, "What you got to ask that cripple for? Is he your momma?"

The very second those words came out of his mouth, the other men who'd been standing around *jumped* out of the way. And kept on running.

When the police came to see him in the hospital, the dumb-mouth joker proved he wasn't a total fool. He told them he'd been so wasted on shine and pills that all he remembered was falling off that rock ledge.

I guess he realized that getting beat up, that's something that can happen a lot of times in a man's life. Getting killed, that only happens once.

Shortly after that, I became a kind of permanent employee of certain people. From then on, all Tory-boy had to say was he had to ask his brother first. His brother, Esau.

Anyone who heard Tory-boy say my name, they knew that they were standing in a minefield. And that the only way out was to *back* out.

That was because the people I did various things for needed me for those things. That was my place in the world, doing those things. Murderous things.

The people I did work for knew they would lose my services if anything ever happened to Tory-boy. So they'd spread the word.

Spread it wide, deep, and thick. If you even *asked* Tory-boy to get involved in something that might get him locked up, that was the same as asking for very serious trouble from some very serious people.

Those people didn't do that as a favor to me. They weren't the kind to do favors for free, and I would never have allowed myself to be obligated by asking them.

The way they thought was always the same, and it always applied to every situation. They'd reason it out like this: if Tory-boy ever got himself arrested, who knew what he might tell the Law, a simpleminded boy like him?

So they kind of looked at people threatening Tory-boy the same way our dogs would. If anyone hurt Tory-boy, there was no guessing to be done—they knew what I'd do. And they didn't want me doing it.

That wasn't out of regard for me; they were just watching out for themselves. They knew I was a professional, and part of that is being extremely careful—it might take me weeks just to put a plan together. But killing someone who hurt my brother, they knew I couldn't wait on that. Worse, they knew I wouldn't care what it cost, or who got hurt in the bargain.

They'd seen that for themselves, the first time we ever met. The time I put in my job application.

My plan finally came true. That's because it *was* a plan. Not some dream, not some prayer, some actual thing I made happen all on my own.

I knew this the same way I knew about my balance. If you wanted to think the spirits spoke to me, I wouldn't call you a liar.

We had to get our own piece of ground. Bought and paid for, cash money. No landlord means no rent—no rent means no excuses to stop by.

Tory-boy didn't really understand why our own land made us

safer. As far as he was concerned, as long as the Beast couldn't get inside, a trailer was as good as a palace.

I didn't have any real use for the library anymore, not with the Internet. But I still went over there at least once a week.

I could have asked myself why, but I was afraid of the answer I'd get.

A man has obligations. Some he asks for, some he gets put on him. Tory-boy, there never was any choice: if I didn't raise him, he wouldn't get raised.

I had to be honest with myself. Had to admit that, somehow, I always knew. When you're birthed out of your own sister—when her father is your father, too—you know you're not going to come out right.

Not you, not your life, not nothing.

So I just worked Tory-boy even harder. Sat him in front of our big-screen and made him watch the news with me, hear how people said things.

He always wanted to please me, and he never got bored, so he was coming along, little by little. It got to the point where I wasn't worried about people knowing he wasn't right the minute he opened his mouth.

One of the most valuable things I taught him was that he never had to say much—in any crowd, there's always someone who wants to do most of the talking.

But no matter how much work I put into Tory-boy, I stayed worried over how he'd handle life on his own. And I knew the day was coming when he'd have to do that.

I accepted the burden and vowed to shoulder it. I knew if I ever fell down Tory-boy would hit the ground right after me.

And I knew I couldn't carry him the full distance. I didn't know when the day would come, but the knowledge that it *was* coming drove me on. The closer I got to that day, the harder I drove.

No matter what, I had to get Tory-boy ready to live on his own. The doctors told me I wasn't going to have a long life. Not even with the right diet, no smoking, the exercising Tory-boy loved helping me with. Under the best of circumstances, I shouldn't count on ever seeing fifty.

But Tory-boy would. And he'd spend the rest of his life in this hard, hard place. Even the coal they dig out of the ground is hard: anthracite, not the soft bituminous kind that doesn't fight the pickax for every chunk. Bituminous burns better, too. You'd think, the harder you have to work for something, the more valuable it would be. But that's just not true. Not around here, anyway.

There's a Klan, but it's not much. Mostly old men who tell wild stories about the things they used to do.

Nobody really listens. Not because folks necessarily disagree with them, but because it doesn't take long for the stories to get as old as the men telling them.

Hate comes easy . . . and it's a lot easier than working. But you won't hear any scare-stories about illegal immigrants in this part of the country. Who'd *want* to come here? This whole place is just one big prison. Some get sentenced to hard labor, some have it easier, but everyone serves the same term: life.

Even the church people don't think about getting out, just about getting by. Like I said, that's got a special meaning around here. And the church people, they do a lot of nice things for folks while they're waiting for . . . whatever they believe is coming to them, I guess.

There's a number of ways you can get respected in these parts. I don't mean feared—that's as easy as grabbing a red-hot weld with your bare hand. Holding on to it, that's another story.

You make people scared enough of you, those same people will watch you get shot down in the street and swear on the Bible that they never saw a thing.

Some of them might even be the shooters.

Fear can make a man run home. But he might be running home to fetch his rifle.

Keeping your word, that's how to get respect. But if you look deep enough, you can see that's not one bit different from being feared. A man known for always keeping his word, if he says he's going to get you, you respect his word by being scared.

Everybody will claim they respect any woman who's a regular at church, but they don't mean a lying word of what comes out of their mouths when they say it.

A woman like Miss Jayne Dyson, nobody respects her out in public. But men who wouldn't say "good morning" to her face are the same ones who knock on her door at night.

I never would act like that. I'd be the worst kind of hypocrite if I did. Who knows better than me that a person can't always choose their own path? It's how you walk that path that makes you worthy . . . or not.

So, when Tory-boy got to the right age—I didn't need a calendar to tell me that; I could see it rising in him—I helped get him ready for that, too.

I could never be sure what Tory-boy had seen when he was just a small child, and I couldn't have the Beast be his teacher. So I paid Miss Jayne Dyson to show him what to do, and how to do it right.

The first time I visited her house, I think she was kind of, I don't know, shocked to see me.

"You're Esau Till, aren't you?"

"Yes . . ."

"Well, yes what?"

"I was going to say 'ma'am,' but I didn't realize you'd be so young. And I don't know you to be calling you by your first name."

"You're Esau Till, all right," she said. "Folks don't have manners like yours anymore. But that is what folks say about you, that you're a true gentleman. Well, you better come in quick, before those nasty old crows across the way start making up stories."

I rolled myself into her parlor. It was real nice, a lot nicer than any home I'd been in myself. She was walking ahead of me, twitching her hips like I'd seen mares do when they're in season.

"You want a little—"

She turned around. Her face was blushing so bright I could see it even in the dim light. "Oh, I'm sorry. I was going to say . . . I mean, just out of habit . . ."

"I understand," I told her. Even though I had no idea what had made her turn red like she had, I've found saying those two words pretty much always works to calm a person when they're upset.

She told me she'd be a lot more comfortable if I'd call her Jayne, instead of Miss Dyson. I said I'd do that proudly, if she'd do the same for me.

Then she said she knew me without ever actually meeting me, so she kind of guessed I knew her, too. Knew what she was known for, she meant.

I allowed that I did, but I made sure I didn't talk to her like she was . . . well, what folks said she was.

I explained why I needed Tory-boy to be educated. I wanted him to learn to treat a woman properly, and I hoped she would help me with that. I did warn her: a young man like him might not know his own strength, especially when he got himself . . . excited.

"Oh, I heard that. I know he's not right in the—"

She saw me looking at her; stopped in her tracks. "Now I *truly* apologize," she said. "I'm ashamed of myself. You didn't come here judging me, and I've got no call judging you or yours."

"Tory-boy's not wise in some ways," I told her, meaning I accepted her apology and it was already gone from my mind. "I hoped you'd help me make him wiser than most in some others."

She smiled at that. That smile, it was so sweet I knew it for a true thing.

Miss Jayne Dyson did a very fine job. I know she did; I know it for a fact. It took a number of visits, but after she was done, Tory-boy not only always had girlfriends, but he never beat on any of them, not once, no matter how they acted.

He never talked nasty to them, either. He knew words could cut like whips. Worse, even. So he always treated his girls like ladies, even when they didn't deserve it.

It turned out that Miss Jayne Dyson, she *was* a lady. Who else but a real lady would have put so much valuable knowledge inside my little brother?

I will never forget the day as long as I live. The day Tory-boy taught *me* something. Oh, what a proud, shining moment that had been for him.

"Esau, did you know that if you treat a girl like a lady, if she really believes you think of her that way—like a lady, I mean—well, you can actually turn her into one!? It's like casting a spell. And you know what else, Esau? I can cast that spell. Me. I never thought I could ever do something like that."

"You mean, you didn't *believe* you could do something like that."

"I . . . Oh, gee, Esau. I get it. I really get it. What Miss Jayne taught me, it wasn't just about girls, right?"

"It's about everything, Tory-boy. How many times have I told you that you're a lot smarter than folks think you are?"

"You're always saying that, Esau."

"And I believe it, too. So that makes it . . . Tell me, Tory-boy, what does that make it?"

"It makes it . . . true! You cast a spell, but it didn't take, because I didn't believe you believed it yourself. I thought you were just being nice to me, like always."

"But now you know, right?"

"I do. I do, for real."

"I would never lie to you, Tory-boy. Never."

He sat down on the floor right next to me and started crying. I patted him like I always did when he was upset, but that time, I knew he was crying for joy.

I was really encouraged by such things. I guess, deep down, I was hoping Tory-boy would find himself a girl with real smarts. A girl he could marry, and then they'd take care of each other. He could bring in all the money they'd ever need—I'd already made sure of that—and she could help him with some of the stuff he couldn't handle so well.

But any girl from around here smart enough to do that kind of thing was smart enough to get out. And never come back.

Tory-boy's mind was always at ease. I kept it that way by surrounding him with knowledge he could have and hold. He knew I'd always fix anything, always keep him safe. Always love him.

I got a lawyer to draw up the papers. A legal trust, so Tory-boy would be taken care of for the rest of his life. I even named the lawyer as the trustee, so he would be the man who paid any bills that might come up. He was also to make sure Tory-boy got whatever else he needed, from bribing a lawman to drawing up a deed.

The lawyer I used, he was a young man. His father and his father before him had been lawyers, too. Now all three of their names were on the shingle, but only him and his father were still alive.

I wasn't worried about that lawyer trying to cheat Tory-boy. His father handled cases for the people I did all that work for, and I was confident he'd passed what that meant along to his son.

If that lawyer ever cheated Tory-boy, if he ever failed on his promises, he was never going to be able to start his car. Or pick up his telephone. Or stand near a window.

He'd never know how or when, but something would be coming for him; he could count on that.

If I was still around, I'd handle it myself. I had a hundred ways to do that. And if I wasn't, then those people I had worked for, their part would be a man with black pantyhose over his face, black latex gloves on his hands, holding a double-barreled sawed-off, with a pistol in his pocket for finishing off his job. The people I had done all that work for, their part was to make that lawyer's ending dead sure.

I didn't care if that ever happened. All I needed was for that lawyer to believe it would.

I had plenty on his father, too. When I told him just a little bit of that, he got real anxious. But I calmed him right down. I made him understand I wasn't selling; I was buying.

All those things I told him, they weren't any kind of blackmail; I was just making a payment on Tory-boy's life-insurance policy.

Tory-boy had more than one of those. Which was kind of the point of me talking to that lawyer at all.

As long as Tory-boy stayed protected, it would be as if I had never died. I'd still be with him, keeping him safe.

We had a car, too. A van, with a lift for my chair. Tory-boy could drive real well. His coordination was damn near perfect. He just couldn't . . . make decisions, I guess is the best way to put it.

So I made the decisions for us both. Anytime I had to deliver one of the devices I made, Tory-boy would always be right there with me. I didn't need him for protection—and I'd *never* let him carry a firearm—I just didn't like leaving him alone.

The people I delivered things to were bad men, but I never felt even a little tremor of fear when I was around them. They were always going to need more of the things I made. And they knew I'd never say a word about them to anybody, ever.

They knew what my word was worth to them. And what their lives were worth to me if they didn't keep theirs.

So I wanted to make sure they knew Tory-boy's face. Had it memorized.

suppose it would be fair to say I was a criminal myself way before I started working for criminals. I was selling those drugs, wasn't I? I knew what drugs did to folks. I'd seen people—kids, even—turn themselves into . . . things. They'd stop being human. Lie to their friends, steal from their own families. Sell their blood and their bodies. Take anything; give up everything.

Drugs. You die from them; you die for them. Either way, you're dead. I knew all that, but it never caused me to hesitate a second.

So maybe it wasn't only my lower half that didn't feel much of anything. Maybe my conscience was like that, too. Not dead, but . . . frozen, I guess. Frozen beyond any heat they have on this planet.

I think that was it. From the first time I showed those people what I was capable of, I'd known what I was going to be doing with the rest of my life.

There wasn't anything else. I used to fantasize about what it would be like if we could put my brain into Tory-boy's body. One of us would have to die to make that happen . . . but neither one would ever know which one had.

If that fantasy could actually happen, it wouldn't matter even if we did know. Tory-boy would die for me without thinking about it. The only difference between us is that I would think about it. But I'd still do it.

Fantasy. Wish. Dream. Whatever I called it, I knew it wasn't ever going to happen.

couldn't help noticing how women denied Miss Webb the respect properly due her. Not because she tried to come in here and change things. She never did that; all she ever wanted to do was make things better. No, those women withheld their respect because Miss Webb never got married, that's why. A lady in her position, she didn't have the option of just taking up with a man. You expect that from trash, but not from someone who got themselves an education.

"Nice-looking woman like she is," they'd say, "she doesn't have a man, you know what that means."

In one way, Jayne Dyson and Miss Webb were like sisters. They both showed proud. Never looked away, never let on they'd even heard the whispers. Always kept their backs straight and their heads high.

Jayne Dyson and Miss Webb, they wrapped themselves in their own self-respect, and no amount of nasty little whispering was ever going to crack those stone walls they put up.

Maybe that's how they found their balance, just as I had.

I really and truly cared for Jayne Dyson. Respected her, too. And even before I was grown, I had loved different women for different reasons—like Mrs. Slater, for helping me raise Tory-boy.

But for myself, for me as a man, Miss Webb was the only woman I ever loved.

People are always talking about how you have to make your own way in this world. Pull yourself up by your own bootstraps. Make it on your own.

They'll look at the TV hanging in a corner of some bar when it's showing a black kid being handcuffed. They'll tell each other that it's niggers on Welfare that are ruining this country.

But the checks *they* get, the ones they drink up every month, those get called County Aid, or Disability, or Unemployment . . . anything but Welfare.

Grocery stores would go broke if they wouldn't take food stamps in exchange for cigarettes or beer.

People blame their lives on anyone but themselves. Where we

live, if you want something better in life, you have to take some risks. Maybe that's why the Klan never got any traction around here. People might sympathize, they might even use the same words, but they weren't going to spend their own money to support it.

For me, it wasn't a real choice. I needed something better if I was going to keep Tory-boy safe. We were both collecting Disability. For-real Disability, not the "I hurt my back at work" kind.

Ours was going to keep coming forever. It wasn't ever going to stop, no more than I was likely to start running marathons or Tory-boy to get a college scholarship.

Those Disability checks wouldn't be going away, but I was. And without me to guide things, no matter how much money I could put aside, it would never be enough to keep Tory-boy safe.

Miss Webb would always be on me to use my mind. I could go to college, she'd tell me. And it wouldn't cost me a cent. Just to make her feel better, I took this test she had sent away for. But when she got back the results, that only made her more determined.

So, one day when there was only the two of us in the library, I asked her if I might speak with her.

She looked at me kind of funny. I guess it did sound strange— I always spoke with her. But she got up from behind her desk and walked over to a far corner. Then she took down a big book from a high shelf—one I'd never be able to reach on my own—and laid it open on the table. If anyone walked in, it would look like the most natural thing in the world for us to be talking about that book.

I took that for understanding, so I asked her to please sit down. Sit next to me.

I told her then. I told her everything. I had to do that; it was only right. I just couldn't bear to keep on disappointing her, and the only way to tell her why I would do a thing like that was to tell her the truth.

My truth was a long list of Nevers.

Never leave this place; never go to college; never accomplish anything the world would recognize.

And the worst of them all: never become a man worthy of her respect.

I told her why this had to be. I even told her what I'd been doing to make sure Tory-boy would always be safe.

I stripped it right down to the bone, so there was no misunderstanding: I'd have to do wrong to make things right. I'd been doing wrong, and I was going to have to do more. A lot more. A lot worse, too.

I don't know what I expected, but Miss Webb breaking into tears wasn't on that list. I reached for the fresh-clean handkerchief I always carry with me, but she already had her own out.

She stopped crying after a little bit. Dried her tears off her cheeks . . . but they stayed in her eyes.

"I understand, Esau."

"I know I shouldn't have said anything to you. I know I don't have that right. But . . ."

"Then why did you?"

"Two reasons," I told her. "One is that I'm forever indebted to you. I know I don't come around as much as I once did, and I couldn't have you thinking I didn't want to come. With this Internet we have now, I can do so much research. . . ."

My voice trailed off like a dying man's breath.

Miss Webb looked at me, and she wouldn't drop her eyes. Blue eyes, she had. But not the blue-jean eyes some around here have—a lighter shade. I wouldn't know the name for that color, or even if it had one. "You said two reasons," she reminded me.

"I . . . I don't feel right about the other one."

"Why, Esau? After what you just told me, what could there be left?"

"Telling you that would be the same as telling you what it was. The reason, I mean."

"And you don't have that reason anymore?"

"Oh, no. That's mine, and that's forever. I'll have it until the day I die. Even after, maybe. What I'm saying is just what I said before. I've got a reason, but I don't have any right to it."

"Esau, you're a grown man now, not a child."

"I'm half a grown man."

"Not to me, you're not. You're more man than anyone I ever knew. A man takes responsibility. Takes it and keeps true to it. No matter what it might cost him."

That's when I learned Miss Webb's first name.

Evangeline.

I learned that right after those eyes of hers finally made me admit that I loved her.

When you're known to be a criminal, crime comes looking for you. One day, Tory-boy came into the house. All he said was that Sammy Blue was waiting outside the gate. Sammy didn't want to buy anything; he just wanted to talk to me about something.

Sammy Blue knew I sold drugs, but that was all he knew. He didn't have a clue about the real work I did, or who I did it for. There was no way for him to have known I was just about ready to get out of the drug business. I'd only sold the drugs when I had no other way to get the money I needed for my plan. But, now that I did, drug dealing was too much risk for too little gain.

But I knew what Sammy Blue did for his money—there weren't too many around here that didn't. So, before I went outside, I put my pistol under the blanket I always kept over my lap.

Tory-boy saw me do that. He knew what it meant. When he came with me to the gate, he wasn't just pushing my wheelchair. The dogs were quiet, but they glared at Sammy Blue hard enough to burn holes through him.

I met Sammy Blue at the gate. I ignored the hand he offered me to shake. I wasn't inviting him to pass through, and he wasn't crazy enough to push the gate open without permission. There were a lot of rumors about what would happen to anyone who put their hands on that heavy wrought iron without getting the okay from me first. Every one of them true.

"Esau, I drove over here—"

"The dogs aren't for sale," I cut him off. "And they're not going in one of your matches, either."

"You haven't heard my offer," he said, smiling like the two-faced, forked-tongue snake that he was.

"You don't have any offer to make me. Those are Tory-boy's dogs. He doesn't want them sold. He doesn't want them hurt. He doesn't want to breed them to anything of yours. What my brother wants is for his dogs to stay here. With him."

"Come on, Esau. You're the one in charge here. What's it matter what that—?"

I couldn't let him finish that sentence. Whatever Sammy Blue had intended on saying died in his throat when he heard the sound of the hammer being pulled back. Maybe I didn't have legs that worked, but my arms and hands are potent weapons. They got built up from all the years of them doing the work they had to do—before Tory-boy came along, and even more later, from taking care of him. Then it was those exercises, all those weights Tory-boy did with me every day. That's how I taught him to count, and now it was a habit. One he cherished.

I held that Colt Python .357 in my left hand. It stayed as cold and steady as the steel it was made from.

"Don't say another word," I told Sammy Blue. "And don't come back. I so much as see you around here, you're dead where you stand."

Later, I explained to Tory-boy that Sammy Blue hadn't followed the rules about the drugs we sold, so I had run him off.

Tory-boy knew I could do that—he'd seen it for himself enough times, even if he couldn't understand how I did it—so I didn't have to explain things any deeper than I had.

If I'd've told my baby brother what Sammy Blue had wanted to do with his dogs, Tory-boy would've walked through the gate, pulled Sammy Blue apart, and tossed the pieces back over the fence. That way, we wouldn't have to bother with burying him.

I couldn't have allowed that. Sammy Blue had too many cop friends—he couldn't have stayed in business otherwise. Like I said, the dogfighting was no secret. Sammy Blue's operation generated cash that went straight to the Law—it was such small potatoes that neither of the two mobs that ran things around here was tapping it for a cut.

In fact, that was the biggest problem with the cops around this way—they weren't as picky as the gang bosses. "Small-time greedy" is how we say it.

One day, the light started flashing in the house. Tory-boy went outside to check for money in the mailbox. But when he came back, I could see he was troubled.

"There's a man out there, Esau. A man in a suit."

"Did he say anything?" I knew Tory-boy could repeat things word for word, provided they weren't too long, or hadn't been said too long ago.

"He said: 'Would you ask Mr. Till if I could have a few minutes of his time?'"

I knew when Tory-boy spoke like that, slow and careful, each word separate, he was as accurate as any tape recorder.

It was good that it had been such a nice warm day. Tory-boy had the dogs trained to let someone through the gate if he told them to. That way I could use the side yard for any conversations I might want to have.

But there wasn't any way the dogs would let a stranger into our house. It was their house, too. That's where they slept. If a leaf fell off a tree in the night, they'd all jump up. No barking, but I could tell by their cocked ears and the fur on their backs that they were ready.

I met the man outside, in the spot that got the most sun. In the nice weather, me and Tory-boy kept a little table and a couple of chairs out there. He especially loved it when it was just the two of us.

If you were to drive by, you'd just see two men, sitting back and sipping some lemonade while they talked. From that perspective, we both looked like a couple of pals shooting the breeze. Maybe that's what he liked the best of all.

But that day, Tory-boy stayed over with the dogs. He was always protecting me. If he saw anything bad happen, I knew he'd rush that man in the suit like a charging bull. I also knew the dogs would get to that man faster than Tory-boy ever could.

And that the sight of a gun pointed their way wouldn't have meant a thing to any of them.

So the man could . . . Well, he could do just about anything he wanted to me. But he'd never leave our property alive, and he looked smart enough to know that.

He had real manners on him, too. Before he took the seat across from me, he said, "My name is R. T. Speck, Mr. Till. I'm a police officer." If standing with his back to Tory-boy and the dogs caused him any worry, he didn't show it.

He held out his hand, and we shook.

"Please have a seat, sir," I told him.

That "sir" wasn't politeness—it was to tell him that I wasn't going to be telling him anything else.

"Would you happen to know a young man by the name of Lonnie Manes, Mr. Till?"

"No, sir," I said. It was the truth.

"I'm not surprised," he said. "We caught this boy—Lonnie Manes, I'm talking about now—we caught him breaking into Henderson's."

Henderson's was what folks called the pharmacy, after the man who'd started it, a long time ago. His name wasn't on the door anymore—the pharmacy had been taken over by one of those big chains a while back—but it was still "Henderson's" to us.

"That boy is about as stupid as they come. If there's one place in town that has top-quality security, it'd be Henderson's. They've even got a central-station alarm in there."

I stayed quiet, but I was secretly proud that this cop showed me respect by not explaining what kind of alarm that was.

"He was after the drugs, of course," the cop said, like saying water is wet. "We caught him walking out the back door with a whole sackful of stuff."

I didn't say anything, but I used my body position to tell him to go on talking. He hadn't driven all the way out here to give me a news report.

"I'm sure you know how police work is done, Mr. Till. I—" He stopped in his tracks, realizing he'd stepped over a line, but he covered up quick: "I mean, from television and all."

I nodded. Even smiled just a little, letting him know I wasn't offended.

"We told Lonnie that he'd been carrying enough drugs in that sack to send him down to the penitentiary for the rest of his natural life. Before we were even finished telling him that, he was telling us about everything he could think of. Everything that might make us go easier on him, I mean."

I just watched the man. The sunlight was strong on his face, and I could see he was older than I'd first thought. I could see right through his eyes, all the way into his brain. My silence was bothering him, so he was considering. Thinking about what to do next.

"You mind?" he said, holding up a pack of cigarettes.

"It doesn't bother me outdoors," I told him, "but I appreciate your courtesy."

He seemed grateful I'd said that. Took him a long time to get his smoke going, even though there wasn't a breath of wind that day.

Finally, he said, "Lonnie gave you up."

I made my whole face puzzled. "I don't understand," I told the cop. "I already said I didn't even know a person by that name."

"The drugs," the cop said, as if having to say it made him sad. "He told us how the whole operation works. Your operation, I'm talking about now."

"I haven't been operated on since—"

That was going too far. I knew it, and I'd done it deliberately.

The man's face got darker. "Your drug operation," he said, colder now. "We know all about that mailbox at the end of your lane. The button. The phone calls to arrange the pickups. Everything. I'd wager, if we were to search your house right now, we'd find enough drugs—"

"Medications," I chopped off his threat. "Anything you'd find in there would come with prescriptions. Legal prescriptions."

"Then you wouldn't mind if I took a look for myself?"

"I don't suppose I could stop you," I said, looking over at Tory-boy. He was standing as rigid as a rock, holding the release lever for the chains. One and Two were standing as well. Three was lying down. They were all staring at the cop's back. "If you'll just let me take a quick look at your warrant, I'll be happy to—"

"That offends me, Mr. Till. I wouldn't come out here with a warrant. That's your home there; I wouldn't expect to go inside unless I was invited. And I wouldn't want anyone else to, either."

"I appreciate that. Then what *do* you want?"

"I already explained that, I thought. Like I said, Lonnie Manes told us everything. We could sit out in those woods with surveillance cameras for ten years and we'd never see you with any drugs. . . ."

He let his voice trail off, so he wouldn't have to say the threat out loud. Tory-boy. If they came and grabbed him, it wouldn't end right. There was no way it could.

"What do you want?" I said again. The cop didn't know his words had just gotten me out of the drug business forever. But he had to know that the limb he'd climbed out on was fixing to snap.

"Lonnie was arrested late last night. That's why I look so raggedy—haven't even had a chance to shave this morning. I'm the only one who took his statement. I'm considered to be real good at talking with people."

"I can see why," I said to him. "But I'm still confused, sir. What exactly do you want?"

"There's no call for looking at me like you are, Mr. Till. What do I want? I'll tell you, right out: I want us to be friends. That's why I had Lonnie write out his statement on separate pieces of paper. What I mean is, separate pieces of paper for each person he informed on. And those pages, they aren't numbered.

"Being entirely truthful with you, Lonnie didn't have all that much. That's because Lonnie *isn't* much. A punk like him, he's not what you'd call a man of his word. You can never be sure when he's telling the truth. Here, see for yourself," he said, pulling a folded piece of paper out of his suit coat.

It was in ignorant scrawl, just the way someone like Lonnie would write it. But a college graduate couldn't have written a clearer account of how our drug business worked. *Had* worked, that is.

"You're right," I told the cop. "There isn't a word of truth in all this scribble."

"Oh, don't bother," he said, when I went to hand it back. "That pack of lies isn't worth a plugged nickel. Might even backfire on the DA if he tried to use Lonnie as a prosecution witness. Put a piece of trash like him in front of a jury, they're not likely to believe a word that comes out of his mouth."

"I can see how that might be true."

"No disrespect, but I don't think you do, Mr. Till. I told you, I came here hoping to be friends."

"A man can't have enough friends."

"Isn't that the truth?"

"Yes. Yes, it is," I said. "And I don't suppose there's any reason why a man couldn't be your friend and sell you an insurance policy, too."

"Now, that's your reputation proving itself, Mr. Till. Folks say you're the smartest man around."

"Would the premiums on this policy be weekly or monthly?"

"I do think monthly would be best. No reason for me to come all the way out here so often."

"How much?"

"Well, I guess it depends on the amount of coverage you'd be wanting."

"I think I'd want the maximum," I said to him. "The full family plan. After all, you never know when something's going to happen, do you? Why only buy fire insurance, when a flood's just as likely?"

"That could end up being a very expensive policy, I have to tell you," he said. "For that kind of coverage, the salesman has to split his commission with his supervisors. All the way up to the top, actually."

"I understand. But that's what insurance is, right? It can't stop things from happening; it just covers you if they do. Life insurance won't stop a man from dying, but it will help his family carry on without him."

"That's true."

"Some folks, they pay insurance on their house for thirty years, and nothing ever touches it. Instead of being upset about all those premiums they paid, my thinking is they should be grateful nothing ever did happen."

"That's the way I look at it myself."

"It just comes down to men being reasonable with each other," I said. "If the premiums get too high, well, then, a man can't afford them, and he lets the policy lapse. On the other hand, if the premiums are too low, the insurance company can't make a living."

The cop stubbed out his cigarette on the ground. Then he took out a little plastic bag, the kind with tops that seal themselves closed, and put the butt inside. It went into his pocket. There's a dozen reasons he could have done that. None of them mattered to me.

"A thousand," he said.

"Once a month?"

"Once a month."

"And that's for *full* coverage? For me and my family? Against anything that might happen to cause either of us any problem with your company?"

"Absolutely total."

"Fair enough," I said, reaching over to shake his hand.

He held on to my hand. Dropped his voice to a whisper. "Folks say you carry a magnum in that left armrest of your chair. Man's got a right to do that. But you won't mind if I look for myself?"

I let go of his hand, leaned back in my chair, and flipped both armrests open.

The cop found the magnum, all right. But he didn't find the tape recorder I knew he was really looking for.

What he did see was about five thousand in hundreds. Plus some of those little packets of alcohol, bandages, stuff that a cripple like me might need.

"You mind?" he said.

I knew what he wanted. Let him feel all over my body, even lift the blanket off my legs.

"I apologize if I offended you," he said. "But you understand—"

"I do understand. And you understand as well. That's all that righteous folks need to make a contract: an understanding between themselves. When one man gives his word to another, it has to mean at least as much as anything you could write down on a piece of paper."

"You have got my respect, sir."

"Mutual."

"I'll be back—"

"One month from today," I told him, handing over a thousand in nice crisp bills, pretending that I didn't see the look of surprise on his face.

That cop drove off, satisfied that we had an understanding between us. We had an understanding, all right. But that's not the same as a partnership.

Which he'd learn only if he did something a lot stupider than Lonnie Manes ever dreamed of. That's when he'd find out that searching me for a tape recorder had been a waste of time.

Around these parts, the one thing nobody is surprised to see on your house is a satellite dish. All the time we were in the yard, talking, that dish was zeroed in on us. When I played back the recording, it was as clear as high-def TV can be. And the sound quality was as good as in an opera house.

I saved it to my hard drive, then I sent it to my coded box, just in case.

If that cop ever turned on me, he'd end up putting his own gun in his mouth. Even if he needed some help to do it.

Like I said, I was already out of the drug business the second that cop had opened his mouth. But I had my plans, and having a tape of him not only taking a bribe, but outright admitting he had to cut a whole lot of higher-ranking cops in on such a take, that could be well worth the money.

The insurance money, I'm saying.

Two different mobs pretty much had things around here all divided up between them: gambling joints, strip clubs, loan-sharking, protection coverage, and, of course, the tax collections.

The white-lightning guys were even smaller potatoes than the dogfighters, but that's not why they never paid taxes. There's folks around here who'll tell you there's nothing like shine—hits you harder than anything you could buy in a bar. But there was no real money to be made from it, and the only men still in the business, they were old men.

And those old men, they kept to the old ways, too. They were very seriously opposed to paying tax. Didn't matter who came collecting. Racketeer or lawman, he might well be buried on the same ground he was dumb enough to cross without permission. If you wanted to visit, the only way to make sure you'd be leaving would be to leave their business alone.

For the two mobs, the dividing line was where County Road 22 crossed Route 76. It was as clear as a border crossing with armed guards: 22 ran north and south, and each mob had its own side, east or west. If you wanted to set up an operation, what you paid was the same on either side, but who you paid was determined by where you wanted to set up shop.

There was some poaching, of course. Not enough to start a full-scale war, but more than enough to get more than a few men killed over the years.

Whoever crossed the line, the mob they came from would always say they were freelancing. That's what stopped things from ever getting out of hand. Even if one mob knew the other one was behind the poaching, they didn't have to take all-out vengeance to hold their pride.

Around here, vengeance and pride are mated so close they can't be separated. If someone does something to you and you don't get back at them, nobody thinks too much of you. It's even worse if someone does something to your family and you let it go. Then you couldn't hold your head up ever again, not even in church.

Poachers, that's one thing. But outsiders, there's a whole different story. Actually, it was outsiders who showed me the way I could make enough money to keep me and Tory-boy safe.

Maybe that's an excuse, I don't know. It's what I felt at the time, but maybe there was something else driving me. That frozen conscience, it could have been. Or all that studying I did early on, about how to kill the Beast. But I never speculate on what I can't change.

The real truth is that the Disability alone would have kept us safe. Add the money from selling my painkillers, that would have done it, easy. But our drug business was doomed even before that lawman showed up and sold me that insurance policy.

What I always told myself was that all I needed was to have money put away. But, inside me, I knew there never could be enough, not without me around to make it work.

That lawman's visit kind of changed my perspective. He started me thinking about getting my hands on so much money that it could push buttons on its own—like setting an alarm clock, or programming a computer.

I thought about that a lot.

The outsiders who opened the door for me were a motorcycle gang. They set up shop on the East Side, in an old airplane hangar. At one time, that hangar was used to house small aircraft, and have work done on them, too. There was a landing strip and everything. But when more and more people got used to being out of work, that business had starved to death.

Later, some company had tried to set up their own airline. Just four-seaters, going over the mountains once a morning, returning that same night. But it didn't take, so they took off themselves, leaving the building there, just rusting out.

I guess this motorcycle gang—MM-13, they called themselves—had just moved into the empty space.

At first, you hardly noticed them. They never bothered anybody when they rode through town, and they didn't often do that. They didn't tear up any of the bars, they didn't try and muscle in on any of the strip joints.

Not only did they behave themselves, they always spent some money, too.

But then they started a meth lab.

At first, the meth had a hard time making a real impact. It seemed like it just wasn't going to take hold. But as time went by, more and more junkies switched over to it. Maybe because it was new, but more likely because it was so cheap compared with any other stuff.

The bikers were about as mobile as you could get, so they sold on both sides of the line. They were too smart to refuse whenever they would run into a tax collector from one of the mobs, but that would only happen by accident—they didn't have regular routes, and they didn't sell out of any one place.

Even if a deal could have been struck, it was impossible to figure out how much the bikers should be paying—they made the meth themselves, so there was no import risk. And they could make it cheap—the street price was so low even the longtime dope fiends were moving over to it.

Anyone could see a showdown was brewing. When the bikers rode into town, there was never more than a dozen or so of them. But if you looked close, you could see it wasn't the *same* dozen. And more and more bikers were moving into that same hangar.

The reason the bar was called the DMZ was because it was the one place where both mobs felt safe. Just west of 22, but the West Side mob never claimed it. There had to be *some* neutral ground, some place the bosses could get together—especially if there was an election coming up. And the only way to make a spot truly neutral was to split the take from it.

So the DMZ paid both sides, but no more than if they were paying just one. The gangs split that money, and put it around that if you started any trouble in there, you were on your own.

Even if somebody got themselves killed in the DMZ, any vengeance was strictly left up to their own people, not their mob.

Getting the bosses to both come there and meet with me—now, that was tricky. But there was no choice about it. I had to put my proposition to the bosses themselves, not go through any message takers.

So I left the exact same word with each mob. I knew they'd check me out first, and that was fine. They'd learn two things: Esau Till might be a crippled man, but he was a man of his word. And he was not only a for-real outlaw—he was smart. Real smart.

The boss of the East Side was Everett Lansdale. He looked like a man in his fifties who took care of his body—one look at his face and you'd see why he thought that necessary.

Jackhammer Judakowski ran the West Side. He was an older guy, pretty well larded—but only a fool would judge his character by his body instead of those ice chips he had for eyes.

I didn't know Judakowski's real name. Around here, folks would say "his Christian name," no matter if he'd never been baptized, or even set foot in a church.

There were a dozen different accounts as to where the "Jackhammer" had come from. One thing I learned, if you want the true history of something, you can't pay attention to what people say today; you have to talk to people that were around at the time.

Another thing I know: old folks don't get a lot of company.

Every time I'd have Tory-boy drive me over to where Mr. Barnes lived, he was always glad for the visit. It was from listening to other old folks that I knew what he'd been called back in the day: Big John Barnes.

The church people came by his place every day with a hot meal. Otherwise, he couldn't have taken care of himself. The church kind of kept up his house, too.

His back was bent pretty bad; he had to stay stooped over all the time. His legs were gone, too. His wheelchair was a lot fancier than mine. More like a little electric scooter, actually. The Medicare people paid for it.

I tried to get by there no less than once a month. I'd sit and talk with him, while Tory-boy took care of anything around his house that needed fixing. The first time Mr. Barnes saw Tory-boy go after some high weeds with a machete, his mouth just dropped open in amazement. "Damn me," he said, "that young man works like the Grim Reaper when he's taking heads."

"Tory-boy is some kind of strong," I agreed.

"I'm not talking about strong, son. You could see that much just looking at the size of him. What I meant was how he's so . . . relentless, the way he goes about it. That's the only word I can think of. That brother of yours, you give him a job to do, he is not going to stop until he's done."

"No matter what the task," I agreed, again.

"Am I boring you, son?" he asked. He never failed to ask me that. And I'd tell him the pure truth: that I loved learning above all else, and I was learning from him. He searched my eyes for truth, every time. Always got the same answer, too.

It took a while, but I finally got the story of how Judakowski came to be called "Jackhammer." I thought it would be some kind of mining story, but Mr. Barnes put the lie to that one. "That boy did it himself. Just started calling himself by that name. When he would be introduced, he'd say his name was Judakowski—Jackhammer Judakowski.

"After a while, it just stuck. You know how, when a man looks the part, he gets the chance to play that part? He does that good enough, a name he gives himself can end up sticking to him like it was on his birth record.

"Of course, the best kind of name to carry is one you didn't make up for yourself. It'd be one people decided to call you, all on their own."

"Like 'Big John'?"

The old man wiped at his eyes. "That was true," he said, real soft. "That was true once."

"I know that, sir. Everybody says it."

He looked at me for a long minute. Then he asked, "And what do they call you, son?"

"You know how people around here are."

"Yeah. Yeah, sure, I know. Nasty and mean in their hearts, some of them. But not all, son. Not all. Never forget that."

"No, sir."

"You still haven't told me what names they—"

"'Crip,' that's one. And 'Half-Man.' And—"

He held up a big callused hand like a traffic cop telling me to stop. "They called me 'Big John' because that's what I was. A big man, name of John. It fit, so it held. For a long time, anyway. What would you want folks to call you, son? 'Brains'—now, that would fit.

"Kind of funny, when you think on it. Anyone who wouldn't call you by a name that truly fit, it'd be the same as naming themselves. You know, something like 'Retard,' or"—I was looking down, but I could feel his eyes burning at me—"'Half-Wit.'"

I looked up. "It doesn't matter," I said.

"What do you want folks to call you?" he insisted. "Not just to your face, either."

"Esau," I told him. "Esau Till."

"Mark me," the old man said. "The day will come when folks will *all* be calling you by that name, son. And by no other."

Y̶ou'd think a man named Judakowski wouldn't hold much sway around here. It was a foreigner's name, and folks put great stock into how far back your name went. Far back local, I mean—not far back like European royalty or anything like that.

Lansdale, now, that was a name that carried weight. His father had been a prizefighter before the War. That was his last fight— one he never came back from. And that counted heavy around here, too.

What opened doors for Jackhammer Judakowski had nothing to do with his own family trail—a Polish name can trace back only so far around here. But nobody would ever be looked down on for having a Polish name, either—not in a part of the world where the name Yablonski is held sacred.

A man who died for his people.

Tony Boyle had been head of the UMW. And the United Mine Workers may have done some violent stuff, but that was only to force mine owners to allow the union in.

People knew that, and they stayed with it. Even when a whole mob had backhoed out a pit, thrown the owner in, and filled it up again—this was down in Tennessee—the jury had acquitted them all.

It might have gone on like that, but when a mine blew up in West Virginia, the truth came out. Boyle had personally told everyone that mine was union-certified, with a perfect safety record. But when the inspectors—federal inspectors—dug through the wreckage and found a slew of major safety violations, there was only one possible explanation: Boyle had been getting paid under the table to sell out the miners.

And it couldn't have been for just that one mine.

That's when Yablonski challenged Boyle for leadership of the union. He called Boyle's men nothing but a gang of thugs, and he promised to return the union to the miners.

When he lost that election, Yablonski said it had been rigged. I don't mean some whispering in a tavern; he said it right out loud, for all to hear.

He was getting ready to go to court to challenge the election results when Boyle had him murdered. And not just Yablonski, but his wife and daughter, too. When the murder team came calling, everyone in the house had to go. No witnesses.

That made it worse. Much worse. Folks who normally wouldn't spit on the Law let them past the wall of silence just long enough to say a few things.

The people Boyle had hired to do that job, one of them had been by Yablonski's house before, scouting. But Yablonski knew he was living under the gun, so he'd written down the license number of that stranger's car.

One by one, they all got caught. The more they talked, the higher the trail climbed. Nobody wanted to chance the Death House.

Their testimony was overpowering. One of them, a girl, I believe, she even had a photograph of the man who had done the hiring shaking hands with Boyle.

After all that, Boyle still only pulled a life sentence. Didn't matter, really—he died in prison.

He would have died even if the jury had acquitted him, and he knew it. Probably why he tried to kill himself. With pills, like the miserable coward he was.

Ask anyone around here and they'll tell you: if Joe Yablonski had lived to be President of the United Mine Workers, things would be different today. They believe that the same way others believe in Jesus. Held that faith just as strong.

Maybe even stronger, now that I think on it. The only way folks could know Christ had died for them would be to read something written down maybe thousands of years ago . . . and believe nobody had tampered with it since.

But to know Joe Yablonski had died for them, all they had to do was read the newspapers. Or listen to someone who was around at the time.

You can't find a living person who claims to have met Jesus in person. Not outside an asylum, anyway. But there's plenty still around who'd met Joe Yablonski. Some who knew him personally. Even some who had been close to him.

And they all tell it the same way.

Once I worked out what I needed—once I decided that there was no other way to get it—the die was cast.

I chose those last words with care, as you'll see.

On the day that started it all, Tory-boy wheeled me through the door of the DMZ, then went back to the van and waited. Just like I told him.

It was broad daylight, and the parking lot was almost empty, but Tory-boy didn't question why I wanted him to park so far away from the front. It did take quite a bit of work to get him to accept the other part, which was: if I didn't wheel myself out of that building, he was to get himself home first, and then call a number I'd made him memorize.

It wasn't a number I could program into his phone, and that puzzled him some, but he proved to me he had it in his head.

And he didn't question why I asked him to recite me that number, over and over again. Or why I asked him to recite it one more time before I rolled myself off.

I made sure not to look back. If I didn't return, I wanted Toryboy to have the image of how much I loved him showing on my face forever.

Once inside, I used my hands to get myself over to a big table where both bosses were sitting, each one in between two of his own men. The empty space across from them was for me; they knew I wouldn't need a chair.

"You each got a note from me," I said, polite but not nervous; it was too late for that. "And by now, you know you each got the same note. I'm not playing one side against the other, and I never would. But I know you've got at least one problem you share. A new problem. And I'm the man who could make that problem go away."

"Why would you want to do that?" Lansdale asked. There was nothing hiding underneath his voice; he sounded like a man asking a reasonable question. Which, considering the circumstances, it was.

"For money," I told him. Told them both, actually.

"How much money?" Judakowski asked, showing me the difference between the two bosses as clear as if he wrote it on a blackboard.

"That's not important right now," I told them both. "That's because I don't want to just solve this one problem for you. What I want is steady work, the kind of work either of you might need doing. Never for one against the other, though."

"The kind of work that solves problems?"

"Yes, sir," I said to Lansdale. I could see Judakowski nod out of the corner of my eye, but when he turned to me, his voice was hard.

"You didn't come here for some friendly conversation."

"No, I came because I can fix the problem you both have," I said, letting a little iron into my own voice. "That problem is a motorcycle gang. They call themselves MM-13, which is a name nobody ever heard of. So it's probably not any kind of national club, just a bunch of men using the motorcycles as cover. My best guess is that the 'M' stands for 'money.' And the thirteenth letter of the alphabet, that's an 'M' as well. Money-Money-Money—that about sums them up.

"Now, I may be speculating on that, but I'm sure of this: they're cooking up crank in that old hangar, and it's cutting into your business. Both your businesses. Meth is cheap to make. So they can sell it cheap, and still turn a fine profit.

"That's why that gang keeps adding reinforcements. They know, sooner or later, you've got to come for them. Neither of you is the kind of man who lets someone take anything away from you."

"There's somewhere around forty of them there already," Judakowski said. I could hear the tiny trickle of interest as it seeped into his voice. "Plenty of military stuff, too."

Lansdale didn't ask him where he got that information. But he didn't argue with it, either.

My turn: "Like I said, that's the kind of problem I can fix."

"How would you be doing that?" Lansdale asked. His voice was as polite as mine. Respectful, even.

"I can make it disappear."

"The man asked you how," Judakowski said. Now his tone was back to where it had started. But it wasn't me he was playing top-dog games with; it was Lansdale.

I sat there for a few seconds, deciding. Then I told them: "I can blow it up. The whole hangar, with all of them inside."

"What're you gonna do, wheel yourself up to the front door and toss in a grenade?" Judakowski said, not even pretending respect.

"Even a grenade wouldn't blow that whole thing up," Lansdale put in, as if Judakowski's crack had been an honest question. "You'd need dynamite, something like that. So how would you get that much explosive inside their place?"

"You know that big empty barn about a mile or so south of here? That farm that got foreclosed on about a year ago?"

They both nodded.

"If you take me out there, I'll show you."

"Planting dynamite in some empty barn—"

"I don't think that's what this man wants to show us," Lansdale said.

"Count me out," Judakowski said. "I got better things to do than wheel some crip around to watch a show."

"No, you don't," I told him.

"You know who you're talking to?" one of Judakowski's men said to me. He was a big guy with eyes squeezed tiny from all their surrounding flesh.

One of Lansdale's men—I later learned his name was Eugene—slid his right hand into the pocket of his jacket, like he was feeling around for his cigarettes.

"It doesn't matter who I'm talking to," I said to the whole table. "I can't have one of you thinking I work for the other one—I know how that story would end. So either you both agree to let me show you what I can do at the barn, or everybody's story ends that same way."

"Now you're gonna blow this whole place up?" Judakowski kind of sneer-laughed.

"See for yourself," I said. Then I pulled up the right armrest on my chair.

Lansdale moved his head an inch or so. The man to his right got up and walked over to where I was sitting.

"It's . . . it's packed with dynamite, boss."

Before anyone could say anything, I closed the armrest. Then I said, "The other side's packed just as deep. Enough explosive to send this whole place into orbit."

"And you're saying . . . you're telling us, we don't go along to see this little 'demonstration' of yours, you'll blow us all up, yourself included?" Judakowski said.

"That is what I'm saying," I told him.

"You're bluffing. How do we know it even is dynamite you've got in there?"

In a way, that was funny. I'd only used dynamite because it was something any of them would recognize on sight—I can cause a bigger explosion with stuff I could fit into a pack of cigarettes. But all I said was, "You know my name. I'm a man of my word. Always. Ask anyone. And I need money. Not just a payment; I need a supply of money coming in, steady. You, both of you, you're my only path to that.

"When I say 'need,' that's just what I mean. If I can't get what I need, I'm not going to be able to protect my brother after I'm gone.

"I know what's going to happen to me. That can't be avoided. And it'll be coming along soon enough. From where I sit—and, yes, I know what that means, too—if I can't protect my baby brother, my time might just as well come right now.

"I mean no disrespect, but if you think you're looking at a man who fears death, you're not looking close enough.

"So it's down to one word. 'Yes'—we take a ride together and I show you what I can do. 'No'—we all go out together. And you won't like that ride."

It was quiet for a long minute.

"I say 'yes.'" Lansdale spoke first. Right then I knew he was the more dangerous of the two—Judakowski didn't want to lose face; Lansdale didn't want to lose lives.

I didn't care if they saw Tory-boy driving me away. I wanted them to know him by face anyway—that was part of my plan.

When Tory-boy stopped the van, a car pulled up on either side of it. And a few more behind.

Probably just out of habit on their part—I didn't need any reminders that I had put myself all-in.

After Tory-boy wheeled me out to the ground, it was my show.

"How far away from that barn you think we are?" I asked the only two men who counted.

"It's a good quarter-mile," Lansdale said, shading his eyes as he looked across the field.

"That far enough away, or you want to move back?"

"Move back," Judakowski said. I could tell he was saying it just to be saying something, but it didn't matter. Not to me, and not to Lansdale, either—I could see that right away.

"How far do you want?"

"Back to that clutch of trees," he said, pointing.

I nodded to Tory-boy. That was our signal for him to push my chair. It was rough ground, hard to navigate. I could have done it myself easily, but there was no value in letting them see how strong my arms were.

He pushed me over to where Judakowski had pointed, then turned my chair around. I took out my range finder. Before I dialed in the coordinates, I held up this thing that looked like one of those mini tape recorders with a little propeller built into it. I'd built it for checking wind speed and direction, and it was never a tick off.

I wasn't in a hurry, but I wasn't stalling, either. I think they could tell that by the way they all stood ringed around behind me. Off to the sides, quiet as tombstones.

"Watch," I told them all, even though I could tell they'd never once taken their eyes off me.

I removed a model airplane from under the left armrest of my chair. I made sure the propeller spun as easy as if it was housed in light-oiled Teflon—which it was. Then I started the motor. The little airplane buzzed in my hand like an angry wasp.

I let it go.

The plane rose almost straight up, then arced and went into a dive, so fast you could barely follow it.

They all watched as my invention hit the barn. And then they couldn't see anything but a red-and-orange fireball rising right up out of the ground.

Fire in the hole, everyone around here has seen something like that. Or at least what it leaves behind.

But when the fireball smoke cleared this time, there was nothing to see. Nothing at all.

One of Lansdale's men ran over to where the barn had been. He was a big, heavy-built man, but he moved at a nice trot, covered ground fast. When he came back, he wasn't a bit short of breath.

"There's a hole in the ground big enough to bury a fleet of semis, boss."

Lansdale looked down at me. I mean that physical, not personal. I don't know if he'd looked down on me as a man before that day, but I knew he'd never do it from then on. None of them ever would.

"That big hangar those bikers took over, it's not really theirs. Doesn't belong to them, so they can't go to the County for utilities," I told him. "Probably running all their electric off a generator. Heating a place that size, they've got to be using a lot of propane tanks."

"So it'd look like—"

"Yes, that's right," I cut him off. "And everyone knows about meth labs. The way they're put together, they blow up all the time."

That was the beginning of the steady employment I'd bet my life to get.

I always tried to keep the two bosses separated as much as possible. Not just in my mind, but from each other. Men like that would always stay suspicious of each other—my only goal was to keep them from getting suspicious of me.

Even though there was a world of difference between Lansdale and Judakowski, they were both in the same business, and killing was part of that business. They weren't killers for hire, but they wouldn't draw the line short of that mark if you interfered in their cash flow.

Either one would have you killed in a heartbeat, but only if you forced them to.

In fact, that was one of their business cards: a reputation for killing anyone who crossed them. That's a reputation you can only get from passing the same test a number of times. There's always wolves watching the campfire, smelling that meat cooking.

But, like I said, they weren't a bit alike. Two people can do the exact same thing; it's only when they have a choice about it that you know the truth about who they really are.

There was an understanding between us: either one could summon me anytime, but they could only send a message, never a messenger. Nobody could come to our house. Anyone who did that, he'd be coming as a stranger. And treated like one.

One night, I was called over to the DMZ, which meant both of them needed something done. I had Tory-boy roll me inside right across from them. Then he took up his post, standing a little behind me, like always.

Before anyone even started talking about the job, one of Judakowski's men got up and walked around behind us, probably looking to get himself a drink from the side bar. I didn't see how it happened, but I did see that man suddenly go flying across the room like a big sack of flour tossed down from a truck.

He hit the wall so hard his neck twisted. You could see he wouldn't be getting up on his own. Probably wouldn't even want to.

Three of Judakowski's men jumped up. I saw Lansdale shake his head "no." Just in time—Eugene already had his hand in his jacket pocket.

By then, I'd learned that Eugene didn't smoke. Didn't carry a gun, either. But I'd seen him work, and I knew what he'd been reaching for. One night, two men got off their bar stools at the same time. They started to walk over to Lansdale's table. Slow and casual, but anyone in our line of work could see what they intended.

It was like Eugene just disappeared from his chair and re-materialized standing on the floor. By then, one of the men had pulled a heavy length of chain from inside his sleeve, and the other was bringing up a pistol.

Eugene left them both on the floor, paralyzed. They'd started bleeding out before either one realized he'd been cut.

I didn't see any signal from Judakowski, but his men all sat right down. Not even pretending they were sorry to be doing it, either.

Then it went quiet. I reached back and patted Tory-boy, making sure he'd stay still.

Finally, Judakowski said, "That Roddrick boy, he always had cement for brains."

Lansdale nodded, as if he was agreeing with Judakowski's wisdom.

That was a nice touch. Just right. Swept any pride issue right off the table.

Judakowski turned to his own men. "How many times have we seen that fucking moron pull that same stunt? He had—what?—fifty damn feet of room to walk in, but, no, he just had to pull his shoulder-bump number on the . . . on Esau's brother. Yeah, good fucking luck with *that*."

"Tory-boy just thought he was shielding me," I said, taking even more of the pressure out of the situation.

Judakowski's men were like he was: hard and strong, no doubt . . . but way too prideful. Seeing how they acted that time, that's what taught me that ego would always be the unseen enemy in any room they entered.

I was grateful for that knowledge. A man's ego can be a real weakness. And the worst kind of weakness is one you don't know you have. Like a man who thinks four-wheel drive works on ice.

"Damn!" Judakowski said. "What would he do if he thought someone was actually going after you?"

"Anything," Lansdale answered, watching me close as he spoke. "Any damn thing at all."

I nodded. It was the truth. But the unseen enemy that infected all Judakowski's men surfaced anyway.

"You think he could turn a bullet?" one of them said. That

branded him as the kind of man who always has to say something, when even a born fool would know it was the wrong time to say anything at all.

He'd put his sneer-question to me, but it was Lansdale who answered again, all the time keeping his voice as calm as if he'd been asked directions to the highway. "*Turn* one, no," Lansdale said. "But a bullet wouldn't stop him, either. Shoot that young man when he's already coming at you, that'd be like giving Eugene a butter knife and locking him in a cage with that Chainsaw Massacre guy. Eugene might get himself sliced up some, but old Leatherface wouldn't be the one walking out."

"You know a lot about him, do you?" Judakowski said to Lansdale. Everyone knew he wasn't talking about Eugene.

"I know what happened to the Lawrence boy," Lansdale said. "You know, that dimwit the cops found with his spine snapped?"

"Tree fell on him, right?" Judakowski said.

"That's what the coroner ruled," Lansdale half-answered him. Smiling just a little bit now, like he and Judakowski were sharing a private joke.

I remembered that day. I don't know how much money might have been bet. Or maybe the whole thing was nothing more than trying to show off for some girl. I've seen men die over less.

What had happened was that the Lawrence boy just walked up to me and dumped over my wheelchair. Same way the Beast used to.

Maybe Tory-boy still had a memory of that, or maybe he just couldn't have anyone hurt me. I never asked him why he snatched the Lawrence boy up in his two hands, held him way up high, and broke him across his knee like a stick of dry kindling.

Everybody scattered as though they were running from a burning building.

I wasted a few precious minutes convincing Tory-boy he had to go back to our place and wait for me. He didn't want to leave me out there all alone, and he couldn't figure out how I could get home without him driving me. I knew he'd obey me, but I wouldn't resort to that. I never let him see the urgency I was feeling, just stayed calm and reasonable, soothing him with my voice. He finally drove off.

Took me another hour to get people over there to drag the Lawrence boy into the right spot, close to that big dead-inside oak, then to loop chains around the tree and pull it down.

I paid well for that work. The men I called expected that, just as I expected them to forget they'd done it.

"That true?" Judakowski asked me. He didn't like Lansdale knowing anything he didn't know himself.

"I only know what people say," I answered. "And you know how some people'll say all kinds of things, just to be talking."

I think Judakowski understood what I was telling him. In fact, I'm sure of it, because, instead of getting belligerent, he just said, "Your brother's got some temper."

"Tory doesn't have any temper at all," I told him. "He's the same as any man—you act like you're fixing to hurt his kin, he's going to hurt you first."

"What if he makes a mistake about that?" Judakowski said, watching me close, knowing he was baiting me about Tory-boy not being known for his intelligence.

I swallowed the bait and spit out the hook at the same time. "It might be he could do that," I said, shaking my head a little, like the thought made me a little sad. "Wouldn't change anything, though."

"I wouldn't be so sure about that. If your brother were to make that kind of mistake, the man he makes the mistake on, might be he'd have kin, too."

"I don't believe there's anyone around here who'd take it that way," I brushed off the threat. "Folks know Tory-boy's judgment might not be so good, so they always cut him some slack."

"Is that right?" Judakowski said. It wasn't a question, not with the sharp edge he put on it.

"They know me, too," I went on, like Judakowski hadn't spoken at all. "They know my brother would never hurt anyone out of meanness, so I've got a right to expect them not to blame him for making a mistake."

"You do, huh?"

"Yes, I do. People know my brother, so that should guide their conduct. People know me, so that should guide their conduct as well. If anything ever was to happen to my brother, they know I wouldn't have to be nearby to settle that score."

"Hell, everybody knows that," Lansdale said. Not to back me up, to push Judakowski away from crossing the line. Giving him an out.

Now, that's a truly dangerous man, I remember thinking at the time.

I was never proved wrong on that.

I didn't spend any of the new money when it started coming in. Not at first. What I did, I invested it. First thing was to build myself a machine shop. We had to make the house easier for me to get into, and easier to move around in, too. For that, we needed all kinds of power tools to cut wood and metal.

But that wasn't complicated work. Once I showed Tory-boy how, he could handle any of the tools. If I showed him a pattern, Tory-boy could cut it perfect.

My lab was another story entirely. I had some tools in there, too. Not for heavy work; just the opposite, in fact. The kind of work I couldn't teach Tory-boy.

Even with the switch that would turn our satellite dish into a signal-sender for the string of blasting caps buried just under the surface out in the yard—buried so shallow you could see them sitting inside the clear Lexan box I built to house them—there was still the chance that enemies could get at us. That's why the metal gates were wired. That's why we had the dogs. That's why . . .

I never underestimate people. What one man can build, another man can bypass. I didn't need to stop enemies, I just needed to slow them down. They might get past everything I'd put in their way, but they couldn't do that quickly enough to ever separate me and Tory-boy, or to stop us from getting down to our mine.

Everybody around here knows something about mining. It's part of our life, in our heritage forever, even though the only nearby mine had dried up years ago.

So when I told Tory-boy we were going to have our own mine— our secret mine—he got all excited and real quiet at the same time.

If I say it myself, I've got a microsurgeon's hands. And my eyesight is so fine it'd put 20/20 to shame—I'd never needed glasses, even when I built some of my most tiny little devices.

I'd disliked working while lying out on the floor—I don't feel completely safe unless I'm in my chair, I guess—but this time it was something that just had to be done.

And I had Tory-boy to protect me while I was doing it.

I'd have him lift me out of the chair and put me on the floor, facedown. Then I'd pull myself over to wherever I needed, so I could do the close-up work on the wood floor of our house.

You'll find some kind of carpet or rugs in just about any house around here, but not in ours. We'd had Mr. Shane come over and lay in genuine wide pine flooring. He's an old man now, retired on that little government check, but his hands still know what to do, and he was as glad for the cash as I expected he would be.

Or maybe what made him glad was me telling him he was the only one I'd even consider for the work I needed done. If he couldn't oblige me, I'd understand, but it would be a deep disappointment, I didn't mind saying.

I knew he'd tell people about the work he'd done on our house, but that didn't matter. After all, I was a cripple, wasn't I? Imprisoned in that wheelchair for life. It only made sense that I wouldn't want to be sliding a wheelchair over rugs all the time.

My work was to undo some of Mr. Shane's work. I was very slow and very careful about it. When I finally finished, you couldn't see where three of the boards had been removed and then put back unless you got down there with a magnifying glass.

Tory-boy loved helping me with my work. And, this time, I wasn't making up a task just to build up his confidence. I could never have moved those heavy boards myself without scratching them up bad, so I truly needed him.

But where I needed him most was when we dug our own mine. It was slow work. We couldn't take out more than a few dozen bucketfuls a night. I made sure Tory-boy knew to scatter that dirt around different trees. The next rain would mix it up perfect, and rain's one of those things you can count on coming, sooner or later.

It took almost two years, working like that, but we built our own little mine.

If I were ever to roll my chair over a certain spot, the boards would come loose, and I could pry them the rest of the way up with the hook at the end of my stick.

A side-railed ramp would take me down to the bottom. Then all I'd have to do is pull the boards back into place with the loops we have fastened underneath. To look at it, you'd never know anyone was under that floor.

Down below, there was room enough for me and Tory-boy. And enough bricks of plastique to excavate a mine shaft.

That was the final exit for us both. If things ever got so bad outside that I couldn't fix it, our private mine is where we'd go.

We'd wait until the house was full of the people who'd be hunting us—we'd be able to hear them right above—and then Tory-boy and me, we'd leave this dirty world behind us.

We'd leave together, but we wouldn't go out alone.

I promised Tory-boy I'd never let anyone hurt him. And I'd keep that promise, no matter what it cost anyone else. A debt is a debt, and an honorable man settles his debts. But my promise to Tory-boy is beyond any debt—it's a sacred duty.

There's no way I can ever get to our mine now. But I can still honor my promises and pay my debts.

And keep my Tory-boy safe. Once he pushed that button, nobody could ever torment him again.

Our mine would be used only if everything else failed. I didn't expect that, but I had to have everything in place so my mind could be at ease.

Neither Judakowski nor Lansdale cared how any problem in their territories got solved. When they wanted a problem out of the way, they didn't care if it left in a limousine or a pine box. I didn't have any special taste for killing, so I always tried the softer way.

Tried it first, I mean. When I took a job to move someone, they got moved. My word was a contract, and I never failed to live up to my end, even when that required the end of someone else.

Sometimes, you can get the exact effect you're after without any bloodshed at all. What I learned was that achieving such an effect depended on a lot of different things. Not just how smart the target was, but how much he had already invested, be it in his racket or his image.

Lansdale or Judakowski would give me the name of a man who was causing a problem. Rarely would anyone be causing them both a problem, but even that happened every so often.

Besides the name, I'd also need the right place to have a package delivered—the target's home was always best—and a copy of a return address he'd trust on sight. I can print up an exact duplicate of any label you show me, right down to the bar codes. The next step is for the man to open that package. Then a big *puff!* of talcum powder would float out in a gentle cloud. The only thing inside the box would be a piece of paper, with a typed-out message:

THIS COULD HAVE BEEN ANTHRAX

If the man was smart enough, that would do it.

But maybe the man had himself committed so deep that he'd already built himself some stronger walls. Maybe he'd never get mail at his home, so any package delivered there would just sit unopened until he had someone come by and pick it up for him.

For a man that cautious, a better move would be if his electricity went out late one night. No warning, everything just *snaps!* off.

Now, that does happen around here. Which is why so many folks outside of town keep backup generators. But this man would look out his window and see all the other close-by houses still showing lights.

Before he can ponder that mystery, his phone rings. The house phone, not his cell. The house phone with the number kept in someone else's name, and unlisted to boot.

A mechanical voice says: "It would be just as easy to turn off *your* lights."

Then the phone goes dead in the target's hand. And the electricity in his house suddenly pops back to life.

It wouldn't take that kind of man too long to think over all the different electrical things he uses every day. All the things he has to touch.

That's when he understands that there's people out there somewhere who can touch *him*.

It's a formula: the higher the target's intelligence, the more subtle you can be about sending him a message.

Some people are just plain mulish. Science can do a lot of things, but there's no cure for a man's personality.

That threw me at first, and it shouldn't have done so. I'd seen too many times how a man's ego can take over everything else inside him—make a usually accommodating man as stubborn as a tree stump.

That's why I always delivered my messages direct into the hands of the man I got paid to fix. I learned the force of ego not so much by reading as by watching. I'd learned that if a man gets warned off in front of his crew, he's never going to act reasonably. It's almost as if he *can't* do that.

I could always get the job done. No matter what it took, I knew where to find it. Or how to build it. All I ever needed was certain knowledge I couldn't get on my own. Knowledge of the target, I mean.

My preference was always for precision. There's no reason to blow up a whole schoolhouse just to kill the principal. That's why I needed the best possible knowledge of the target . . . so I could decide on the best method to make him go away.

I turned myself into a persistence hunter. The fastest animal on earth is a cheetah, but there's a tribe that kills them for food. They can't outrun a cheetah, but they can keep running long after the cheetah can't draw another breath. Takes them hours and hours each time, but they know, if they stay at it, the outcome is always the same.

When I took a job, it was known I'd stay on it until it was done. How could I charge the prices I did—how was I supposed to keep earning the money I needed—unless my word carried its own worth?

Here's an example of that. I didn't know why Judakowski needed that new preacher gone, but I was assured the Reverend Elias never went to sleep in his own bed without spending some time with his Presentation Bible—the one they give you when you graduate from divinity school.

That Bible was precious to him. It never left his house, even when he traveled. But he had others—whoever heard of a preacher who went around without at least a pocket-sized one? And he was leaving on a two-week circuit soon.

I'm no burglar—that's understood, and such a service is never expected from me—so Judakowski's men had to bring that Bible over to his place for me to pick up.

When I told them they had to take digital photos of that Bible from several angles, including tight close-ups, before they so much as touched it, they gave me a funny look. When I told them I would need the camera they used, too, so I could check to see if they'd done their job right before I started on mine, I felt them getting ready to buck.

"Do what the man tells you," Judakowski said. He didn't have to say any more.

His men were expert thieves, but they didn't know anything about putting stuff *back*.

It was almost three days before I was satisfied with the wire-thin string of microchips I built. But it took me only a couple of hours to drill a tiny hole through the binding between the pages of paper and the spine. Then I threaded the string of microchips through that hole and touched each end with a tiny droplet of nail polish to hold it in place.

When I handed that Bible back to Judakowski, it was open to the same page it had been when it was stolen. I told him his men had to use the blown-up digital shots I'd made to guide them through putting the Bible back exactly where they'd found it. I even drew a diagram for them, with all the measurements in inches.

I also told him they had to handle that Bible like it was made of spun glass. Most important of all, they had to be absolutely sure not to close it.

When I say "fix," that's just what I mean—solve a problem. That's why Judakowski never hired me for one of those blood feuds he was always getting into—that's not the kind of job you can outsource.

Lansdale never seemed to have those kinds of feuds. Whenever he hired me, it was to move someone aside who was standing in his way. Business. Nothing personal.

That's why I was so taken aback when he called over to the barmaid one night, "Bring Esau his usual, will you, Nancy? Uh . . . better make it a double, okay? We've got a lot to talk over."

Everyone who worked in Lansdale's joint knew I only drank apple juice—not even cider, pure juice. They always kept some on hand for me. Fresh, too.

I didn't show it, but that meant a lot to me. Not the juice itself, the way they respected the decisions I made about my own body.

The first time I'd ever come alone to his bar, Lansdale had

asked me what I'd have. Didn't bat an eye at what I told him. Ever since then, I could count on a big mug of apple juice being brought over to the table whenever I visited.

What had taken me aback was that Lansdale asked the barmaid to bring me that drink *after* we were done talking business. That made it clear that he didn't want anyone else hearing whatever it was we were about to talk over.

Neither of those things had ever happened before.

"Thank you," I told the barmaid when she brought my drink.

"You might be the only man who ever brings his church manners into a bar, Esau," she said, flashing me a grin. "But don't be leaving me any more of your tips. I warned you about that, didn't I?"

"You did," I admitted. "But I can't just—"

"What, call me Nancy? Trust me, I've been called a whole lot worse than my own name."

"It's not that," I told her. "It's just that . . . well, you being a young girl, it seems like I'd be taking liberties, doing that."

She put her hands on her hips and stood there, her eyes searching my face.

"It's been a long time since anyone called me a young girl, Esau. You know why I choose to work here? It's the one bar in this whole lousy town where they don't allow drunks. Mean drunks, I'm talking about. And nobody's ever crazy enough to start a fight in here. But the best thing of all is that every man who walks through the door knows buying a drink doesn't give him leave to paw the help.

"Most of the men in places I worked before? Far as they're concerned, when they buy a drink, pinching the serving girl's ass is included in the price."

"I didn't know that" is all I could think to say.

"No," she said. "No, you wouldn't. You're too smart for that, aren't you?"

"Smart?"

"Oh, come on! A man's been around as much as you, he knows a rich silver tongue works better than a cheap gold bracelet. On a real woman, that is."

Right about then, I was grateful for the soft lighting in the bar. And for the even darker pool of shadow where Lansdale kept his personal table.

"The way I see it," Lansdale said, "you ain't got but two choices, Esau. And little Miss Nancy here, she's famous for her stubbornness."

"With your permission, then," I said to her.

"With your permission, *Nancy*," she corrected me.

"Nancy," I surrendered.

"You're missing the show," Lansdale said to me as Nancy walked away. "That girl can flat-out bring it."

"I don't—"

"Tell you what," he said. "Roll on over to the side, next to me. And empty that drink, Esau. That way, you'll see exactly what I mean when Nancy brings you a refill."

Lansdale was right on that score. In fact, I downed a whole lot of apple juice that night.

Just as well I did—Lansdale had a story to tell, and it wasn't a short one.

"You've heard of Casey Myrtleson, I take it? To hear folks talk him up, you'd bet that young man is going to set NASCAR on fire one day. Sure, he's kind of wild, but nothing wrong with raising a little hell when you're still in your twenties. It was our own people who really got NASCAR started, and you know how they learned *their* driving skills—by now, it's in our blood.

"But a young buck like Casey Myrtleson, he doesn't just drive fast, he does everything fast. Stirs up a whole lot of rumors in his wake."

"I suppose he might," I said, not having even a clue as to where all this was going.

Not that I cared. I would have been content to sit there all night.

"You and me, we're the same," Lansdale said. Not like asking a question, stating a fact. Before I could ask him how he could possibly think such a thing, he told me.

"A man can put up with a lot of things. Some more than others. But there's a bottom to every well, and a man who won't protect his own, that's not a man."

"I'd never argue that."

"Just think of the lengths you'd go to to protect your little brother, Esau."

"You can't have lengths for that."

"Why do you say?"

"Lengths means there's a limit."

"And you're saying, when it comes to protecting your own, there is no limit."

"That *is* what I'm saying," I told Lansdale, fear of some threat to Tory-boy already darkening my mind.

But then he went off in another direction entirely. I knew he had two children, a boy and a girl. And I knew his boy was a real terror in his own way—a newspaperman who got the Klan mad enough to burn a cross in front of his house over some articles he wrote when he was first starting out. The paper he wrote for now, it was the biggest one in the state, published in the capital. That was a long way from here, so I didn't imagine his father could protect him much.

Anyway, Lansdale was peacock-proud of his son, but I could see he thought of him as a grown man. Old enough to pick his own road, and already walking it.

Not so his daughter—she was still in high school. One of those special-blessed beauties. Folks could legitimately argue over which was more lovely, her church-choir voice or her movie-star face.

"I do admit I worry myself about her," Lansdale said. "A girl her age, she's likely to be impressed by the wrong things, you know what I mean?"

I just nodded, so I wouldn't be stopping him from talking.

"Judgment, that's something you have to learn," he said. "Some never do. Take that Casey Myrtleson we were just talking about. Now, he can burn up a racetrack, for sure. Thing is, he's full-grown, but not yet grown up. Keeps on taking chances, just to be doing it.

"There's chances a man shouldn't ever take. You can bounce your life off the rev limiter one too many times—there's a reason why they paint red lines on tachometers."

"A warning."

"Now, that is exactly what it is!" Lansdale slapped his hand on the table hard enough to break it. "But there's always going to be men like Casey Myrtleson. They see a 'No Trespassing' sign, they figure they just found themselves a fine place to go deer hunting."

That's when I finally understood what Lansdale was really talking about. "Man like that, he'd probably take a doe out of season, even if he had to jacklight her," I said, just to make sure.

Lansdale looked me full in the face, like he was trying to read something written in a language he knew a little bit, but not to where he'd be called fluent.

"Good talking with you, Esau," he finally said. "I know we do business, but I hope you regard me as your friend, because that's how I regard you."

Casey Myrtleson was big stuff. And going places, too. But he hadn't gotten there yet, and he wasn't so big that he didn't open his own mail. Especially a pink-wrapped box with little red hearts all over it.

A few weeks after, I rolled into Lansdale's bar. I'd spent those weeks listening to the stories. It seemed like Casey Myrtleson being blown to bits was all folks could talk about.

They had it every which way the mind could imagine. Casey had been using cocaine to sharpen his reflexes and ran up a big debt in the process. A certain driver Casey had put into the wall a few times had made sure that wouldn't ever happen again. A wealthy old man's young wife had told too many stories at the beauty parlor. Casey had been trying to brew up his own mixture for the track, and playing around with nitro-mixing fuel isn't for amateurs.

On and on. After a while, I swear there were more stories than there were people telling them.

As I came in the door, Lansdale stood up and walked over to his table. Nobody else was there. Nobody would ever *be* there unless Lansdale himself had invited them over.

Somebody stepped behind me and took hold of the handles of my chair. I didn't understand that, but it didn't worry me, considering where I was.

That night is so fixed in my memory that I can recall what was playing on the jukebox when I saw Nancy coming over to me:

> *I used up all my pity on myself;*
> *Ain't got one bit left for no one else.*

Only this time she wasn't smiling. Not even close. "Just what in hell do you think you're doing, Elmore?" she said to the man behind me.

"I was just trying to help—"

"You think Esau needs *your* help to get around? The man's got arms on him like thick lumps of iron."

"Now, how would you be knowing that?" the man Nancy had called Elmore said to her.

"And how would that be any business of yours?" she snapped back.

Before he could say anything, Lansdale stood up and waved me over.

hank you, Nancy," I said when she put the mug of apple juice in front of me.

"Let it go, now," Lansdale told her. "The way you're fuming, you'll give yourself a damn stroke."

"Where does that bucktoothed white trash think he—?"

"Nancy," I said, "could you do me a favor?"

"I . . . Sure, Esau. What would you like?"

"I'd appreciate you asking that Elmore fella if he'd come over here for a minute. I know he tried to do me a service, and I'd like to shake his hand."

She stole a quick look at Lansdale. He nodded his head, giving her the okay.

Elmore came on over. He was a big guy. Not Tory-boy's size, but over six foot, easy.

I offered my hand. He took it.

It wasn't five seconds before he called it off.

"Hah!" Nancy said to him. "I told you—"

"Could I get one more of these?" I asked her, holding up my empty glass.

"You can get anything you want, honey," she said, and planted a little kiss on my cheek before she walked off.

I don't know where Elmore went to. Me, I was in Heaven.

"You are truly something else, Esau," Lansdale said, shaking his head like he'd just seen an amazing sight. "Your spine may be all messed up, but you got enough backbone for a tribe of gorillas."

I didn't want to reply to that, so I just waited for Nancy to get back, then held up my glass by way of saying "thank you" to Lansdale and Nancy both.

Lansdale had been right about the beauty of how Nancy walked, and I hadn't missed an opportunity since. As soon as she was out of sight, Lansdale offered his own hand.

It was a man's handshake, firm and strong, but nothing like that foolishness Elmore had tried.

"There isn't a liquor store in the world that lets you buy on credit. So, if a man walks into a liquor store after dark, it's either because he's got money . . . or because he doesn't."

"That's why they all deal from behind that bulletproof glass," I agreed. "Because, just looking at a man walking in, there's no way you can tell."

"Unless you know the man," he said, holding up his square-cut whiskey tumbler.

"Unless you know the man," I said, tapping my mug of apple juice lightly against his glass.

"My wife and I, we'd be honored if you and your brother would take supper with us Thursday night, Esau."

That hit me like a shock wave of . . . well, I don't have a name for it. That invitation was beyond anything I'd ever expected to happen in my life. And including Tory-boy, well, that was exactly the way such things are done—you invite a man for dinner at your home, you invite his family, too.

Treating Tory-boy like he wasn't "special" was the most special thing anyone had ever done.

"I'm truly honored by your invitation," I said, keeping it as formal as a tea dance, "but I'm also honor-bound to refuse."

"Why would that be?" Lansdale said. His voice was as polite as mine, but I could feel something darker lurking around its edges.

"It's not right to accept an invitation when you can't reciprocate. Our place isn't suitable for a man to bring his family to."

"You think I don't know that?" Lansdale said, all the darkness suddenly gone from his voice. In fact, he was outright grinning at me. "No offense, but I don't know anyone in this whole county who'd accept an invitation to have a meal at your place, Esau. More than likely, they'd think you were inviting them to *be* the meal.

"You know how people talk. There's all kinds of horror stories about those dogs of yours—supposed to have a real taste for human flesh, the way I hear it."

"Not a word of truth to that," I said, feeling the smile come out on my own face. "But they really do fancy the organs."

"So you're saying—?"

"Pardon the interruption, but I couldn't wait to say this. I accept your kind offer, sir. And the honor would be ours."

Lansdale had a fine house. Nothing showy, but you could see it had taken real craftsmanship to put it together.

The only thing that didn't go perfect was when I had to touch my finger to my cheek, the signal for "Stop it!" Tory-boy had been staring at Lansdale's daughter like he'd been hit over the head with an ax handle. A whole bunch of times.

Not that I really blamed him. Patsy was every bit as beautiful as folks said. But I'd taught Tory-boy better than that. And not just for politeness' sake—gawking at a girl gives away too much information about yourself.

There's much better ways to pay a compliment. Such as when Lansdale's wife insisted that I call her Kay. Later on, I told her I was a man who'd studied science all my life but it didn't require a deep knowledge of genetics to see where Patsy had taken her looks from. I could tell she knew I wasn't slick-talking, just telling the truth in a polite way.

"You'll always be welcome here, Esau," Kay told me at the end of the evening. "You and Tory come on back anytime you get tired of eating your own cooking."

"I can cook," Tory-boy immediately piped up.

"Oh, I'm sure of that," Lansdale's wife said, as she reached out and patted Tory-boy's forearm. "I don't imagine there's much you couldn't do if you put your mind to it."

It was right there that I learned the difference between just having good manners and having genuine class.

acquired some of my knowledge late. But after working for a time, I came to understand that everything in life always boils down to principles.

Principles come in two forms.

Some you can never change, like a scientific principle that had proved itself, over and over again. That reliability test: x always causes y.

It's the "always" that makes it science.

The scientific principle for making a bomb is as logical as not scratching a poison ivy rash. All you need is a container that isn't strong enough to hold whatever you put inside of it. The stronger the container, the stronger that inside force has to be.

Another scientific principle is that accuracy will defeat firepower. One truly skilled sniper could wipe out a whole gang, provided he had good enough cover and plenty of time. A tiny dash of poison in a cup of coffee could take down a man powerful enough to bend a crowbar in his bare hands.

But inside that principle there's another one, which you can't see. No matter how powerful the explosive or how potent the poison, they're absolutely worthless without a direct-delivery system.

You want to kill a powerful man with poisoned coffee, you have to get him to drink that coffee.

The other type of principles are those a man chooses to live by. No man can change scientific principles, but any man can change his own.

How else could there be traitors?

Lansdale had made himself an enemy. He didn't know who it was—although I suspect he had an idea—but he knew someone was committed to his death.

"It came out of nowhere," he told me. "The box I was sitting on slid just a tiny bit, the side of my face felt this little bee-sting . . . and *then* I heard the crack of the rifle. I dropped and rolled behind some rocks, but it was another few seconds before I realized I was bleeding. Whoever he was, he didn't miss by much."

"You were in Grant's Tomb?"

"That's right," he said. "Now, how would you guess something like that, Esau?"

So that's why he wanted to meet, I thought to myself. Part of me was saddened that he might think such a thing. I had been a guest in his home, and I was sure he knew how much that had meant to me.

I promised nothing but truth in this record, so, even though it shames me to admit it, another part of me was offended. If I'd been sitting behind that sniper's scope, I wouldn't have missed.

But all I said out loud was "That box you were sitting on, sliding a little like it did, that probably saved your life. You said you didn't hear the sound of the shot until after you felt it kiss the side of your face. That means it was fired from a long distance—half a mile, minimum. There's no shortage of mountains around here, but they're all covered with leafy trees, especially this time of year. That's how I figured it had to be Grant's Tomb—where else could a sniper get a clean shot at you from that far away?"

That calmed him down right away. I could see it on his face as he followed the trail I had reasoned out.

The trail actually started about fifty or sixty years ago, depending on who you ask.

A big-time strip miner named Silas Grant had a vision come to him. Lots of folks have visions, but Silas Grant had piled up enough coal money to actually chase his vision down.

Gold, that was his vision. A vein of gold so thick it would take you a day just to walk across it. So much gold that it made the Mother Lode look like her baby.

Silas Grant spent his whole fortune trying to find that gold he saw in his vision. He bought up hundreds of acres, set up his mining operation, and built a whole little town around it. Years and years went by. Folks said the workers dug down so deep they could feel the heat of Hell.

But Silas Grant died without ever extracting anything but tons of rock so worthless that he even lost money having it hauled away. That's why the folks around here call that spot Grant's Tomb— Silas Grant was a man who worked himself to death digging his own grave.

When he died, that property was about all he left behind. There wasn't any reasonable use for it—just to fill it in and level the ground would cost a thousand times more than the land was worth.

His family was rendered poor. Well, poor by the standards they were all used to. That made them so bitter that they didn't even bother to put on the kind of funeral folks would expect from people of their standing.

For years, the ground stood fallow. The whole mining town ghosted out. All that remained was a bunch of rickety old buildings, a couple of looted trailers, and some heavy equipment that was rust-shut forever.

When Lansdale went and bought the whole site from Grant's family, they thought he was Heaven-sent. He probably hadn't paid all that much, but it was enough for them to leave here and start over someplace else. Someplace where they weren't known.

Nobody knew what Lansdale wanted that place for, but it was no secret that he held meetings down there.

"So . . ." That was just Lansdale, thinking out loud. I kept quiet. I waited in that quiet because I knew he'd ask me questions when he got done with whatever he was thinking through in his head. That had happened so often that I'd come to expect it.

"So it could only be one of two things, then," he finally spoke out loud.

I nodded. When he didn't say anything else, I knew he was waiting for me to spell it out.

"Somebody's camped up there permanent," I said. "Built himself a hide he could live in for months, if he had to. All he'd need was restocking—supplies, food, batteries for his phone and radio, maybe stuff to read. And he'd have to be the kind of man who could handle being alone."

Lansdale nodded. Then he held up two fingers, like making a "V" sign.

There was no sugarcoating the other possibility, so I just said, "Or one of your men is taking someone else's money."

"Or just plain talks too much," Lansdale said. He shifted his body a little, and looked at me real close. "So that's three possibilities, Esau. If you were a gambling man, which horse would you put your money on?"

"Those last two, you're splitting the same hair."

"The same? Come on. There's a million miles between a man who will sell you out if the price is right and a man who can't keep his fool mouth shut when he gets liquored up . . . especially around a woman."

"Still no difference, really."

"Meaning, if he *isn't* camped up there permanent, that sniper had to know I'd be out there that day he took his shot. So, a traitor or a drunk, it still comes out the same?"

"The reason the sniper was in place doesn't much matter—if he'd've hit you, you'd be just as dead."

"I'm trying to be cold-blooded about this," he said, "but I just can't see any of my men selling me out. Or even talking out of turn."

"That's what doctors call a 'rule-out.' One of the football players from the high school takes one of those helmet-to-helmet hits. Knocks him unconscious. Even if he comes to on his own, even if he gets up and walks over to the bench, even if he says he wants to go back in, they'll still carry him over to the ER.

"That's why they perform all those tests—CAT scans and other stuff like that. They have to rule out brain damage. Some concussions, the brain actually bounces back and forth against the inside of the skull. You send that kid back to play too soon, he could end up talking like some of those old boxers do.

"That's the scientific method of working: there are times when you have to make sure what something *isn't* before you can start looking for what it is."

"That sounds right to me, Esau. Ruling out a sniper camped out up there first. That was the case, they wouldn't need an inside man in my crew."

"If you want to know for sure, just take me out there. If you can show me the exact spot where you were when—"

"Nothing's been moved," he interrupted.

"Makes it even easier, then," I told him. "That bullet left a nice trail down the side of your face, but it would have to flatten itself out on the rock behind you. Too much of a mess to tell you much from looking at it, but I'd put my money on it being a NATO round."

"That's like a .22, right?"

"Not much difference in size," I told him. "But a whole lot in speed."

I wonder if he knows? I remember thinking. But I let that thought go. Lansdale was a subtle man, but he wasn't a game player. So I just kept rolling:

"You put yourself in the exact same position, give me some time to work with my instruments, I can probably point you to within ten yards of wherever that sniper was roosting."

"What good would that do me?"

"It'll answer your question. If it was a sniper planted up there, that's a card whoever wanted you dead can only play once. If a hide was built, there'll still be plenty of traces left behind. The sniper fired only once, and you went down right after. He couldn't see you behind those rocks, so a second shot wouldn't do any good—he either nailed you or he didn't. So he probably took off without stopping to clean up after himself. And even if he'd tried to, there's no way he could have covered up the signs a man would leave being up there for that long."

"I'll do it," Lansdale said. He'd started to get to his feet when

I made a little motion with my hand. When he sat down again, I leaned close:

"What I just said only works if the sniper had really been planted there, waiting. You understand? If he *didn't* know when you'd be showing up . . ."

I could tell Lansdale didn't like even the thought of any other possibility. "Yeah," he said. "And so?"

"So, if you go out there, and you don't find a blind, you're as good as telling whoever betrayed you that you're on to him. Maybe not to him, exactly, but you'd still be showing your hand without making him pay to call it. If you know it was someone from inside your organization, would you want them knowing you knew?"

"I can't *not* go out there, Esau. I've got . . . all kinds of business that needs to be done from that place. Hell, that's why I bought it—nobody could get close enough to listen, and there's no place to plant a microphone."

"Can't have your men think you were scared off, either. Or that you might be questioning someone's loyalty."

He smiled at that. "So you've got a plan, do you?"

"I do."

"How are you going to spot a sniper's roost up in all that mess? It could be damn near anywhere."

"I'd need two men," I said. "Not hired hands, men you're willing to trust with your life. I'm guessing that both Eugene and Coy are on that list."

"If I'm wrong about them, I'd rather die than learn of it."

"I understand," I told him. And I truly did.

C oy put me over his shoulder and carried me all the way to where we finally found the sniper's hide. Whoever had put it together had spent a lot of time and effort on the job.

And I was right—the sniper had bailed out after his one shot missed. No point in hanging around. Lansdale's survival instinct had kicked in the second he'd heard the shot. He rolled behind one of the boulders, and all his men had taken cover, too. Some had scoped rifles; they were already scanning. A couple of others had backed all the way out without showing themselves, and the sniper had to figure they were on their way up to where he was.

He'd left plenty of things behind. Nothing that would tell us who he was, but more than enough to catch sun-glints from the refractory mirrors I'd set up for Eugene and Coy to move around every time I told them to.

"A setup like this, he wouldn't need anything but patience," I said.

"Yeah," Lansdale said, "I've got a bit of that myself."

But I could see he wasn't really paying attention. From the moment we'd found that hide, he'd been grinning like a kid who got a pony for Christmas.

"I knew that stupid Polack couldn't wait his turn," Lansdale crowed. "Probably thinks all that's left to do is pay the sniper off with the same coin he deals out, and then everything's his."

"Can you be sure it was Judakowski?" I said, more out of concern for Lansdale than anything else. "Might be more than one person around who felt unkindly toward you."

"Might be at that," Lansdale said, chuckling. "Come on, Esau, aim your own weapon. Use that deadly brain of yours. A man might get mad enough to take a shot at me, sure. But any sniper that patient *and* that professional, he's not going to come cheap. Times are hard. Who's got the money to be throwing around like that?"

If you're wondering about how Lansdale knew I've got what it takes to shoot a man in cold blood, I can tell you how that came about.

It was mid-afternoon when we all heard a car's tires crunch against the pebbled parking lot behind Lansdale's office. In front, it was a poolroom, but it was no secret that the back office was where you had to go if you wanted to do business.

"It's a dark-red Hummer, boss," Zeke said, peeking out between the blinds. "Tinted windows, big wheels. Parked sideways."

Lansdale didn't say anything, waiting on more information. I rolled my chair into a corner, adjusted the blanket over my lap, and slitted my eyes.

"Three men," Zeke said. "Could be more of them in there—that's a damn big ride, and the windows are tinted so dark I can't make out a thing inside."

"Strangers?" Barton asked.

"Niggers," Zeke said.

"Not what I asked," Barton said. He was just as loyal as Zeke, but a whole lot smarter.

"If they know enough to come in the back way, we may not know them, but they know us," Lansdale said. He pointed to his right. Barton stepped into that spot. Zeke went over to the door and opened it, like it had been standing that way all along.

There were three of them, but it was clear there was only one in charge.

"My name is DeAngelo White," he said, talking right at Lansdale, who was still behind his desk. "I came a long way to see you. We can make some money together—serious money, I'm saying."

He hadn't offered his hand. Neither did Lansdale. "Have a seat" is all he said.

As DeAngelo sat down across from Lansdale, his two men moved smoothly to each side, standing like bookends. That triangle-forming move looked so natural you could tell it was something they were used to doing. Even though each of them was outflanked by one of Lansdale's men, they stood relaxed, keeping their hands in sight.

That looked practiced, too. Or maybe they just shared the same overconfidence as their boss.

DeAngelo got right to it. "You've probably never heard of me. I believe you'll agree that's not a bad thing. In fact, it's what you might call a business advantage."

His voice was that of an educated, intelligent man. He spoke like a college graduate, not a thug. I felt ashamed—professionally ashamed—for the assumptions I'd been making since he and his two men walked in the door.

Around here, a dangerous man wouldn't call attention to himself, never mind wear such outlandish clothes and jewelry. A man in my business has to be able to judge dangerousness in others, and overlooking their intelligence is a good way to get yourself killed.

"But I've heard of you," DeAngelo went on. "I know I need to reach an understanding with you if I want to move my product in this part of the state."

"Not going to happen," Lansdale said. "Your people come to these parts, they're going to stick out like the bull's-eye on a shooting range."

"No, man. I'm not talking about some little hand-to-hand stuff. In the business I'm speaking of, you'd be a retailer, okay? Which means you have to get your product from a wholesaler. Now, me, I am a wholesaler.

"All that means is weight; it doesn't say a word about quality. So I came here to give you my personal guarantee that my product is pure. You can step on it a lot heavier than anything you're getting now and you'll *still* be selling better stuff. Despite that, I'll match any price you're paying.

"So far, all I've done is talk. You don't know me, you don't know my reputation, so I understand that I have to prove myself in. And I'm ready to do just that.

"How would it be if I left you a serious sample—I'm talking three keys—completely on trust? You take my sample, you test it anyway you want, then you'll know how much cut it'll hold. After that, you just distribute it. You'll at least double your usual take from the same amount. And you don't owe me a dime until my stuff proves out.

"Now, sure, you could just give me a blank look when I showed up later, looking to get paid. You could say, 'What three keys?' I'll take that chance, because, once you see how much money there is to be made, ripping off three keys wouldn't be worth it. A bad business decision.

"See what I'm saying here? No way you can lose. When you're out of product, you just let me know—we got all kinds of ways you can do that—and I come back with a new load. All you have to do is pay me for the one you *already* made serious money on.

"Now, where else could you find a wholesaler who'd hand over product on trust? That's not the way the game works. But I'm not just a wholesaler, I'm an innovator.

"If you and me can do business, then we both make bank. I get a bigger market for my product than anyone expects I could—and you make more money for yourself . . . a *lot* more money.

"And I don't want to stop there. We can agree to sharing the wealth, sure. But if we increase the wealth, we could end up sharing a much bigger pie. You feeling me?"

It was quiet for a couple of seconds. Then Lansdale said, "I wouldn't feel you with barbecue tongs."

Then it was DeAngelo's turn to go quiet. But not for long. "Yeah. All right, my man. I see where you stand on this. I'm a student who does his homework. That's why I've never taken a fall—I study the situation before I ever make a move. I gave you the respect of making you my first visit. But you know how the game works: one player passes, another one sits in."

"No" is all Lansdale said.

"What is it that you're trying to tell me, man? I already got your answer. Next stop is this guy they call Jackhammer. You're not telling me I can't ask him if he likes my offer, are you? I mean, the way I understand it, you guys aren't exactly cut buddies."

"What I want to hear—and this is the only thing I want to hear—is that you're leaving," Lansdale said. "Leaving now. And not coming back."

"You don't need to be worrying about that. DeAngelo White never goes where he's not wanted."

"I guess I'm not making myself clear," Lansdale said. "I'm not talking about coming back to me; what I'm saying is, don't come back here. *Anywhere* around here."

"Be serious, man. I'm in business. You can turn me down, and I can respect that. But no way you speak for your competition, am I right?"

"This isn't about who I'm speaking for," Lansdale told him, "it's about who I'm speaking to."

"You might not like certain colors; I get that. But the only thing whiter than my own name is my product."

"I wouldn't know that," Lansdale said. "And I'm not ever going to find out."

Something in his tone told DeAngelo that his antenna had been tuned to the wrong station. "People know I'm here," he said. Said it calm, like he was doing Lansdale a favor, keeping him from making a big mistake.

"Who?" Lansdale said. "Your parole officer? I'm not going to keep saying the same thing over and over."

"Not necessary. Neither am I. And when—not if—when I come back up here, I won't be coming with a couple of friends like I did today. You feeling *that*?"

"I am," Lansdale said. He looked kind of sad when he spoke. The instant I saw DeAngelo's two men slowly shifting their outside shoulders, I shot DeAngelo in the back of his head.

The single-shot pistol I used was my own invention. The barrel was as big as a 12-gauge, but that was mostly the baffling—the bullet was the same .220 Swift I like so much, but I'd packed it with far less powder, to keep it subsonic.

The shot made a noise like a puff of air. DeAngelo crumpled to the floor, the slug still inside his skull.

His men froze, not sure what had just happened. It was only for a split second, but that was enough for them to realize Zeke and Barton already had them covered.

"I'm truly sorry about this," Lansdale told DeAngelo's men. "But your boss brought it down on both of you."

"DeAngelo never could make up his mind about what he was. Which means he was guaranteed to overstep his bounds one day," the man standing to my right said. There was no fear in his voice; just a man reciting some facts. "We ain't his partners; we ain't in his crew. We're just men he hired to come along today. That's what we do, hire out. DeAngelo pays good, but he don't *think* good. Likes to put on a show. That's why he had us both facing you. Looks cool, but don't leave nobody to watch his back.

"Like you said, he brought it down on himself. Just something that happened. Got nothing to do with us."

"It kind of does, now," Lansdale said. "I don't bear you any ill will, but I also don't know you. So letting you walk away, that would be a bad business decision. You feeling me?"

Barton and Zeke fired at the same time. Their pistols boomed like thunder inside that closed space.

Zeke got down to check that all three men on the floor were gone. He spent quite a bit of time on DeAngelo. He and Barton had fired heavy hollow-points at such short range that survival wasn't possible, but he had no idea what had taken DeAngelo out.

"I can't see no blood, but this one's gone for sure, boss," he said, his fingers on DeAngelo's carotid artery.

Lansdale just nodded.

Barton came back into the office. "There were three more of them inside that Hummer, boss. The engine was running. Real quiet—probably never turned it off. One was behind the wheel. The other two had MAC-10s."

"Cover fire," Lansdale said.

"Had to be," Barton agreed. "That's why they had the back doors standing open. Just enough so they wouldn't have to waste time piling in."

"I didn't hear any shots."

"With Eugene, Coy, and Adam, why would you?"

Lansdale smiled. Not his usual grin; this was more like just showing his teeth. "If that car of theirs could carry six of them out here, it can just as easy carry them all away. We'll have to flatbed it. Call Delbert. And make sure he brings a big tarp with him."

Men came into the back office and rolled up the bodies on the floor in individual shrouds. It was clear they'd done it before by the way they used box cutters on the room-sized sheet of heavy black plastic that was always under the rugs.

"You want—?" Zeke started to ask.

"Not until Junior runs his blue light over the floor," Lansdale stopped him. "We might have to bleach the wood, then sand it down good, before we put the new rugs in. And we don't want to move the bodies out of here until it gets just a little darker, so you can leave them right there for now."

After the men left, it was just me and Lansdale.

"You're a man of many talents, Esau" is all he said.

After that, the range of jobs I did for him expanded significantly.

It was almost fifteen years before I could make things right with Mrs. Slater. She still lived in that same house, so I was a little concerned about how Tory-boy would react when we had to go back past the place where all those ugly things had happened. But if he even recognized what was left of that burned-out shack, he didn't show it.

I hadn't needed to wait that long to stack up money; it was my timing that had to be perfect. Not only would I have to wait until Mrs. Slater needed something more than just my thanks, I knew I'd be facing some powerful resistance from her.

Lansdale had someone at the bank. That's how I learned Mrs. Slater was a widow. And that her husband hadn't carried any life insurance since he'd been laid off from his last job.

The house should have been paid off, anyway. The way the banks do it, you have to buy insurance from them, so that if you die that pays off whatever's left on the mortgage.

But the bank said the policy only covered the face amount of the mortgage. With all the late charges the Slaters had racked up, plus the interest on that, never mind that they were already some months behind on their payments, by the time they finished playing with their computers Mrs. Slater owed almost three thousand dollars.

Still, she was working, and the bank could have written her a new note. Refinanced the property so that her payments wouldn't be more than a few dollars a month.

But the bank knew real estate was really going up. Rich folks from the big cities were "discovering" towns like ours all over the state. Nice and cool in the summertime, with plenty of fishing.

And with all the work Mr. Slater had put into the house, it was worth a lot more than when they'd first bought it. The vultures floated high, riding the air currents, always watching with great care. They had to be sure their prey was really dead before dropping down to feed.

Foreclosure was the meal they planned on having.

With such a small balance left, Mrs. Slater could have just sold her house and walked off with a profit. But she wasn't going to do that.

People around here, they don't do that. It just doesn't feel right to them.

Lansdale also told me Mrs. Slater had an old Ford. She didn't owe anything on it, but it was damn near shot; probably wouldn't see her through the next winter. Not only that, she had to drive about forty miles a day just to get to the only job she could find after her husband had stopped bringing home a paycheck.

When I asked Lansdale about her children, I admired the way he answered my question. "Never had any" is all he said.

The women around here can be crueler than the men. They can say things that cut to the quick, and they're not reluctant to use that knife. When they talked about a married woman who had no children, they'd always use that sympathy-sounding voice that was nothing but gloating covered with fake skin.

"That poor Mrs. Johnson. The Lord never blessed her with children." That was the nicest way they'd put it.

"It's too bad about Mrs. Johnson never being able to give her husband any children." That was a step up their cruelty ladder, but nowhere near the top.

The meanest—and their favorite—was to just shake their heads in false sorrow whenever they referred to Mrs. Johnson, always making sure the word "barren" found its way into their pretend-pity.

That really made me think on how—"prepared," I guess is the word I'm searching for—on how well prepared Mrs. Slater had been to help me with Tory-boy when he first came.

When we pulled up in the van, Mrs. Slater came out onto her porch. That's the way folks do. No need for a doorbell when your driveway is gravel or chipped stone. Or if you have a dog.

She looked like most of the women around here do after a while: gaunt, hard lines cut into her face. Worn hands, suspicious eyes.

But all that changed when the van's side door opened and the release system lowered my chair to the ground.

"Esau? Esau Till. Is that you? My goodness. And this is—"

"This is my little brother, Tory," I said. "That's why we chose Mother's Day to visit. Had it not been for your saintly kindness, he wouldn't be standing next to me right now. The way I always looked at it, you're Tory's real mother. I've been telling him about you since he was old enough to understand."

She clapped her hand over her heart, like she was about to faint. "My goodness! I'd heard . . . Well, just listen to me! Like I was raised in a barn. Can you sit a spell?"

"Yes, ma'am. I came out here for that very reason. There's something that's been worrying at me for a long time, and now that I've been led to the righteous answer, this was the place I had to come to."

I could see she was puzzled by what I said. And she drew quite a breath when she saw Tory-boy pick up me and my chair the way another man would pick up a newspaper.

He carried me up to the porch; then he pulled back Mrs. Slater's chair for her. I believe that may have shocked her even more—good manners count for a lot around here, but the older folks never get tired of saying that young people just don't know how to act anymore.

Both Tory-boy and me said we'd love a glass of the lemonade she offered. We weren't lying, either—the month of May can get brutal around here.

We each took a little drink, and Tory-boy beat me to telling her it was delicious. I was never prouder of him than that day—there wasn't a single thing he did that wasn't perfect.

When I told Mrs. Slater I was deeply sorry for her loss, she just nodded. I took that for what it was: an acknowledgment, maybe even thanks. But nothing more than that. Showing the truth of herself—this was not a woman who would ever seek sympathy, especially from a man who knew all about suffering firsthand.

Still, me and Tory-boy bowed our heads. A moment of silence for the departed.

She understood without a word being said.

After that, we went back to visiting. In the midst of all the polite talk, I saw the opening I'd been waiting for.

I almost never went to church when I was young. Even the most devoted of the congregation—the folks who'd come and carry you to church if you didn't have your own way of getting there—they never came near our shack on a Sunday. In fact, Mrs. Slater was the only one who had ever dared.

But I've read my Bible and taught myself. I can talk Christian with the best of them. I knew I'd have to call on that skill if I was to succeed on that special Mother's Day. In a way, I was just like the sniper who fired at Lansdale. My intent couldn't have been more different from his, but, like him, I'd only get the one shot.

"Mrs. Slater, the reason I'm here today is because I've done wrong, and you're the only one who can help me put things right."

"What could you have done, Esau?" I didn't get my feelings hurt. In fact, I felt some pride. I knew Mrs. Slater. I knew she wasn't questioning what a crippled man like me could do, not after knowing how I'd raised Tory-boy all by myself. No, she was speaking of my character, of my reputation.

"I don't want to come off as some kind of boaster, ma'am, but . . . well, I'm generally considered to be a pretty intelligent man."

"Intelligent? Esau, you're the smartest boy we ever had come from here. It was in the papers when you won first prize at that Science Fair, and everyone says you're doing so well, earning such good money with your business and all. I'm not sure exactly what it is you do—"

"I'm a consultant, ma'am. It's work I can do from home, and, what with the Internet, I can deal with problems all over the country. All over the world, in fact."

"I am not one bit surprised."

"And I thank you for that, ma'am. But let me explain what I meant about doing wrong. Now, you know what is written: if a man is blessed with powers, he is obliged to use them only for good."

I waited for her nod of agreement—and the confused look on her face that came with it—before I went on.

"Well, the good Lord has blessed me with a fine mind. And I've used that mind to make a good living, for myself and my brother.

"So I had no need for money. But I was tempted, and I fell. Somebody told me about this big poker game they have in town every Saturday night.

"I know I shouldn't have gone into a gambling den, but I told myself I was only curious about such things. And maybe that was actually true, at first. I couldn't say what brought me there, because I honestly don't really know.

"But what I do know is that I ended up studying that poker

game. Not only the game, but the men who were playing. And I kept on doing that, week after week.

"If I had stopped there, if I had gotten bored, if I'd had my fill of the foul language some of them used, or the whiskey they swilled, there would be no story to tell.

"Only, it didn't end there. One night, I brought my own money to that table, and sat down to play."

Mrs. Slater sat there, waiting for me to finish my story. She worked at keeping a shocked look off her face, but she couldn't do anything about her eyes.

"From the second I put my money down on that green felt table, I knew I was doing wrong," I told her. "But my sin was much worse than gambling. You see, I had all the advantages over the others. I know how to compute odds in my head faster than this," I said, snapping my fingers into a sharp *crack*. "And from having watched them so close for weeks, I knew what each man was holding. I could tell by the way they acted when they looked at their cards.

"This is what I mean: one man, every time he's bluffing, he always takes a tiny sip of his whiskey while he's waiting for other people to decide. Another one, he has a little tic in his right cheek that goes off every time he's holding top cards.

"The plain truth is that there was no way I could lose. I wasn't playing poker; I was using a poker game to take money from others. The only difference between what I did and sticking up a bank is that I didn't use a gun.

"I have repented what I did. I know that's not sufficient, and I accept the responsibility of that knowledge. But surely you understand that I can't just give the money back. Not to those people— that would only cause more trouble. And I can't keep the money, either.

"So I went over to see Pastor Knight—I don't know if you've ever met him; his church is way over the other side of town. I was looking for guidance. To be honest, I thought he was going to tell me to give the money to the church.

"But the pastor told me he didn't have an answer. He said such a question was too big for him—it was a question for the Lord Himself.

"I understood that to mean I would have to pray for guidance on my own. If my prayers were sincere, the Lord would answer. And I did pray on this. I prayed long and hard. Time passed—but the Lord finally answered. It was almost as if He was punishing me for my sins, making me prove I was truly penitent before He would show me how to truly atone."

I drank some of her lemonade, as if it was a strength-giving elixir.

"The Lord told me that I must make an offering. Not to the church, but to a person who had both sacrificed greatly and suffered unjustly.

"And then it came to me, like a bolt of lightning in the night. A true vision, it was. I looked back on how you had sacrificed to make sure that I could raise my baby brother. I saw how you had suffered the loss of your husband. . . . God's truth, there was nobody else I could see—the harder I prayed, the more you flooded my mind."

"Now, Esau—"

"Please forgive me interrupting, Mrs. Slater. But Tory and me, we are each bound to ask you to grant our greatest wish. Each of us has a wish, and you are the only person on God's earth who could grant either one."

"Esau, you know if there's anything I can do . . ."

"Two things," I told her. "For me, I must hand this over to you, and I beg you to accept it."

I had the money in one of those oversized yellow envelopes, the kind that are bigger and stronger than the regular ones. I reached it out to her. Reached out to her as I had so many years ago.

The way I put it, she couldn't refuse. I knew that, just as I knew she wouldn't open the envelope until I was gone.

She tucked it into her apron, signifying my part was done. Then she turned to Tory-boy.

Oh, sweet Jesus, he was just perfect. Better than perfect. I swear there was a glow all around him when he leaned forward and said:

"Mrs. Slater, ever since I was old enough to understand, I always called you 'Mom' in my heart. On this day, if you would allow me, I would like to say it out loud, just this one time. It would mean the world to me."

Even though I expected tears, I wasn't prepared for Mrs. Slater crying and smiling at the same time. She didn't say anything, but I nodded at Tory-boy as if she had.

He reached over and took her hand. "Thank you, Mom," he said. "Thank you for giving me life."

We stayed with her for quite a while after that. I didn't think she would ever stop crying, but she finally did. Then she had to hug Tory-boy and kiss him. Over and over.

I hadn't prepared Tory-boy for all this, but he took in every drop of that mother's love he'd been starving for his whole life.

It was the finest day any man was ever blessed with. I can't say it any better than that.

Even if Mrs. Slater had wanted to check into my story—and I knew that was highly unlikely—there were any number of folks who'd tell her that winning $18,475 in one night wasn't anywhere near unusual, not with the stakes those people played for.

She was a strong woman, there was no doubt on that score. When I first heard about her husband passing, I feared what we call "busted nerves." I never heard of a man getting a case of it, but it's not uncommon for a woman who's lost her husband and has no children.

They don't get thoughts of suicide, but you can tell they have no real interest in living, either. Like flat tires with punctures that can't be repaired. Just sad and empty. Sometimes they have all kinds of physical pains, too, but the doctors never find anything wrong with them, so they write them up as depressed or whatever, and they end up on Disability.

I don't know what this place would be without those kind of

paychecks. Probably like that little mining town built all around Grant's Tomb.

The next time we went, Tory-boy took her a gift as natural as you please. Miss Webb had shown him how to make a bouquet from wildflowers, and he'd done a beautiful job.

Miss Webb even looked up the records, so we knew when Mrs. Slater's birthday was.

When Miss Webb told me the date, I wasn't surprised. But when she told me it was Tory-boy who had asked her to find it for him, my hopes for my baby brother took off like a bottle rocket.

Tory-boy handed over the bouquet the next time we visited. "For you, Mom," is all he had to say.

After that, he said it a lot.

Ever since we'd given up selling my drugs, I'd kept Tory-boy a good distance away from crime. I never tried to cut myself in on anyone's operation. I never wanted to run anything. I didn't even want to have anyone working for me.

No crime I ever did was on a contingency basis. I didn't want a percentage share; I wanted to do a job of work and get paid for it. Nothing more, and surely nothing less.

The way it is here, it's not just the poverty, or crooked politicians, or anything else you might want to blame. It's . . . environmental, I believe. An invisible cold gray acid rain that never stops falling.

Around here, even dying can be hard. Horribly hard. Only death itself comes easy.

By easy, I mean frequent. Death happens so often around here that people regard it pretty much the same as that never-ending rain.

When life itself is hard, you have to be hard to live. Even a bitch will cull one of her own pups if she doesn't think he's going to be tough enough—she knows she's only got but so much milk, and there's none to waste.

Around here, survival isn't some skill you learn—it's in all our genes. Nobody needed to be told to step aside when they saw the Beast coming. But not everyone stepped fast enough.

"Hard" isn't the same as "mean." We've got all kinds here. Some of the finest, most honorable folks are also the kind you don't want to interfere with. But they don't give off signals like the Beast did, so a lot of mistakes get made. And people die.

Death is always here. Black lung takes longer than a methane-gas explosion, but they end the same way.

There's always hunters in the woods. The ones hunting for food aren't dangerous, but those hunting for fun sure can be.

Everyone keeps some kind of firearm around. Most carry a knife, others keep taped-up lead pipes in their trucks. There's whole barns full of decomposing dynamite.

The only difference between one Friday night and another is that they're not *all* fatal.

But when they are, if the dead man left kin, you know there's going to be more than one funeral.

Going to prison is pretty common. Coming out a better person than when you went in, that's never been done.

There's rock slides. Floods, too. Those are natural phenomena. You live here, you expect them. But just because a man's found under tons of rock, or floating in the river, doesn't mean his death was due to natural causes.

Folks drink a lot. Wives get beaten something fierce. Some of those wives can shoot pretty good. And some of their husbands never think it can happen to them, even when they're sleeping off a drunk.

Any old man who tells some story about how the town was once prosperous, people just think his brain's gone soft.

I'm not saying that there isn't good in the folks we have here, only that it isn't appreciated like it might be in other places.

There's supposed to be good and bad in everyone. Probably is. But here, it's the bad in you that's more often the most useful.

Like the difference between climate and weather. Most folks around here don't view a killing as good or bad—just something that happens, like a flood or a fire.

That's why a whole lot of bodies never get viewed at all.

For a man like me, this is a good part of the country to do my work. I don't care what stupid book you read or what silly TV show you watch, it never so much as occurred to me to enjoy my work. No more than it would occur to me to work without getting paid.

I did take pride in the quality of my work, but I never deceived myself that every death at my hands was justified, never mind righteous or noble.

I never saw myself as . . . much of anything, really. I was a crippled, cornered rat, trying to protect my little brother with whatever I could use. In the process, I learned a lot of things. But I never did anything without testing it first.

Not everything I experimented with was a success. A lot of that was my own fault. I spent weeks putting together what looked like a pair of clamps. The top clamp had a pair of hollow steel tips on its upper side. And a spring that would discharge venom from the fangs as soon as they closed down.

I knew the width of a mature timber rattler's fangs. I knew how a pit viper delivers its poison, and how deep its fangs would penetrate. I practiced on different slabs of meat. Naturally, full penetration was easiest on fat, harder on muscle, hardest of all on bone.

Collecting some of that venom was no problem. Tory-boy could move faster than any copperhead. After all, he'd been training to move fast ever since he could crawl. Besides, the snakes would usually freeze in position, because that's how they got their prey to come close enough for them to strike—camouflage.

But after all that work creating what I thought would pass

any autopsy test as an accidental snake bite, I discovered that the chances of someone actually dying from a bite were pretty remote. In fact, snake handling was such a common practice—mostly Pentecostal, but other sects did it as well—that it was even outlawed in some areas. Some of the handlers had been bitten dozens of times, and were none the worse for it. Timber-rattler neurotoxin was designed for varmints, not humans.

So, even with all that custom design work, the only time I ever used my invention was on a man with an impressive potbelly and a known habit of going hunting alone. He claimed to have invented a 12-gauge deer slug that was as accurate as any rifle bullet, and he wasn't giving anyone a look until he got it patented.

He had another habit, too. I don't know for a fact that this habit would have bothered Judakowski under other circumstances—it wasn't cutting into his business. But one of Judakowski's girlfriends had a little boy who the fat man was bothering in a real bad way.

"It has to be an accident," Judakowski told me. He didn't believe in warning people off like Lansdale did.

The man's name was Jonah. I didn't know if that was first or last. Or even why Judakowski thought knowing his name at all would be useful to me.

By the time they found that Jonah, all my work to mislead an autopsy turned out to be needless. The copperhead struck so perfectly that its fangs hit a prominent vein on his forearm, and the fat man must have stepped into a bear trap as he tried to run for help.

It's not legal to trap bears, so, the way the cops figured it, whoever set that trap had gone back to check it, seen Jonah caught in it, and faded back into the forest.

They did the autopsy anyway, but they stopped just about as soon as they opened him up—his heart had blown its valves, probably from a combination of pain and fear. No need to look further. He could've also died from loss of blood, but "accidental" was the only possible entry on the death certificate.

Besides, by the time someone stumbled across what was left of him, he'd been out there over a month, and various creatures had sampled his flesh.

"Worth every penny," Judakowski told me as he handed over the rest of the cash he owed me.

I thought it was worth that much to him because his girlfriend would be so pleased with how he'd handled her little boy's problem without going near the police. But it wasn't even two weeks later that she disappeared. Her and her little boy, too—vanished without a trace.

Blowing up those White Power defectives who had tried to take Tory-boy from me wasn't hard. With all the advance notice I got from him about their big meeting, I was able to drop over a dozen of my little black helicopters on the flat roof of their bunker. I had the position dialed in; I only flew them *real* early in the morning, when it was still dark; and they hardly made a sound.

It was the worst kind of luck that the FBI had a man planted inside one of those groups that had come there that night. Like I said, they never would have caught me otherwise.

Why would it have been anything else *but* bad luck? Bad luck had been in charge of our lives from the very beginning. Me and Tory-boy were born under the most evil sign there was.

Don't read me that speech about "bad choices." I had all kinds of bad in my life, way before I had any choices.

Put it this way: once I began, I never minded killing any more than I had ever minded dying. So, if it hadn't have been for Tory-boy, there's no evidence that I would have turned out any different than I did.

But if it wasn't for Tory-boy, I wouldn't ever have gotten caught, either.

They call us—me and the others locked up with me—they call us "condemned men." Some snarl saying it, others sob.

Neither changes a thing.

I once had thoughts about what could have done that—what might have actually changed things? If I hadn't been born bad, if

I hadn't seen things no child should, if . . . if I had been a normal man, could I have courted the woman I came to know as Evangeline? Could I have married her?

Those thoughts almost killed me. I had to make a pyramid of them and set fire to it. Because I don't lie to myself. And I know what I was really thinking, underneath all those dream-thoughts. I was thinking, what if Tory-boy had never come along?

Here's the truth I'm left with: if I hadn't been afraid of losing Tory-boy to those Nazi idiots, I wouldn't have blown up their fort, and doing that is what got me caught.

But there's a stronger truth, and that's the one I hold closest: whatever good is in me, whatever honor I have, it all came from my little brother.

N ow that I think it through—and I do that every night—I realize that's where my train went off the tracks. Not where, actually— more like Why. If I'd stuck straight to business, me and Tory-boy would still be going on just like we always had.

It really started with Judakowski. Jayne Dyson had never told me about the man who . . . did what he did to set her on the only path she was allowed to walk. But after Judakowski beat her to death, it was the same as if she had.

Sometimes, I get so full of how smart I am that I forget there's others just as smart. And when it comes to certain things, a whole lot smarter.

I was at Lansdale's place. After we'd finished talking over some job that needed doing, he kind of casually mentioned how terrible it was, what had happened to Miss Jayne Dyson.

I don't think I showed anything on my face, even when he told me how the cops said whoever did that to her was some kind of animal—tore her up so bad they could tell it was the first time any-one had ever . . . had her that way.

She had horrible bruising on her where no woman should

have. And everybody knew Miss Jayne Dyson wouldn't let anybody do something like that to her, no matter how much they offered.

"I'll tell anyone, Miss Jayne Dyson was a real lady," Lansdale said that night. He looked genuinely sad. "But even if she was . . . something other than a lady, she didn't deserve what was done to her."

I agreed with him. It was no secret that I had visited her a number of times. There's no secrets in the part of town where she lived. But I think everyone assumed my visits were all about Tory-boy.

Lansdale hadn't made that assumption, although I didn't figure that out until later.

"She must've fought like a wildcat," he told me. "I heard Judakowski's face is going to be marked for life."

"Judakowski?"

"Sure," Lansdale said. "I think his last stay in the penitentiary gave him a taste for . . . well, you know what I'm saying, don't you, Esau?"

"Yes, I do. But why would he . . . ? I mean, there's plenty of other . . ."

"That's Judakowski," Lansdale said, shrugging his shoulders. "He's not a man you can say no to, not when he thinks he's got power over you. He's not even denying he did it. See Henry over there?" Lansdale nodded his head in the direction of a man sitting at the bar, his back to us. "He was in the Double-J a couple of nights ago. Judakowski has his own table, naturally, but Henry was close enough to hear him say, 'You can't rape a whore,' like he was reciting a verse from the Good Book.

"Of course, nobody argued with him. A man'd have to be crazy to do that in Judakowski's own place, especially when he was all liquored up."

Then Lansdale went back to talking about other things.

When I called and told Judakowski there was something I wanted to talk over with him in private, I could see right inside his head. Judakowski was the kind of man who thought he knew the whole world just because he knew himself so good.

I could see him thinking I was going to offer to take Lansdale out if Judakowski would make me a partner. He knew that respect was really important to me, so he figured maybe I was sick of being paid by the job.

If he was right—and Judakowski would never even imagine otherwise—I wouldn't want anyone else to hear me make that kind of offer; it would be too risky.

Judakowski himself was always looking over his own shoulder. He didn't trust everyone in his own crew. And if he didn't trust people who worked for him, why would I trust them myself?

What he didn't figure on was me wheeling over to where he was sitting on a big tree stump in that clearing, working on a cigar. I wheeled over close enough to see his face. I had to see for myself those marks Miss Jayne Dyson had left.

"I'm proud of you," I said.

Judakowski knew I wasn't talking to him. But before he could open his mouth to ask a question, I shot him in the face. Right at the bridge of his nose. I didn't want to spoil those rip scars on his cheeks if they decided on an open-casket sendoff.

The shot hardly made a sound. And nobody was ever going to trace the bullet in Judakowski's brain to the gun in my hand. I'd made that pistol myself; I knew how to unmake it just as well.

I rolled up even closer. Then I held his head back by the hair and put two more bullets into his head, one for each eye.

It was peaceful and calm in that glade. The birds kept on singing while I laid the pistol in my lap and took out my wire cutters.

I left Judakowski's tongue on his chest. More puzzle for the cops to solve, maybe. But, for sure, plenty enough to start lots of other tongues wagging.

I'm not spiritual. But I know Miss Jayne Dyson watched every move I made.

"Thank you," I told her. "Thank you for everything. I swear on my brother, if I had known what was in his mind, I would have done this before he ever had a chance to hurt you."

All Tory-boy knew was that he drove me to where I told him, and waited by the van for me to come back. He didn't know who I was meeting up with, much less why.

I guess someone might be able to trick things out of Tory-boy, if they asked the right questions. That's why I'd always made sure to keep that kind of distance between what I did and what he knew. How was anyone going to make him tell what he didn't know?

I'd attended to Judakowski no more than a few weeks before when I was snatched up for atomizing those skinheads, or Nazis, or whatever they were calling themselves now.

Maybe I'm rambling now. Not being precise, the way I like to be. All of this is a lot of stuff to put down on paper. And, like I said, things around here never seem to happen in a straight line.

I guess it's obvious by now that I killed Judakowski for my own reasons. And it's even obvious that Lansdale had known that telling me how Miss Jayne Dyson had been raped to death had been signing Judakowski's death warrant.

So now it's time to tell the Why of that.

I once thought about my body and my mind as a single unit. That sounds strange, maybe—my mind can do all kinds of things, and my body can't even carry me across a room. But what I'd been thinking about was the frozen part. My conscience should have stopped me from doing some things, so I told myself that it had just stopped working, as atrophied as my body.

"Atrophied." I hated that word as much as I loved "inertia." Once you start rolling, you stay rolling, true enough. But if you never use something, it just . . . rots. Only Tory-boy wouldn't let my legs rot. He'd grab my ankles and just work my legs. It hurt a bit, but I remember it like a treat. A treat I'll never have again now.

I'm just dancing around the perimeter, and I know it. So here's how it happened. I was over to Miss Jayne Dyson's one afternoon. That was the way we worked it; if Tory-boy had a question that a woman should be answering for him, I'd call Miss Dyson and make an appointment. Then we'd drive over there.

I always left them alone. I knew it would be easier for Tory-boy that way.

He was in her little parlor a good half-hour that time. It takes Tory-boy a while to get something down. But once he gets it, he keeps it.

I just waited on Miss Dyson's porch. I knew people could see me out there, but it didn't bother me a bit. None of those spike-tongued women would ever be talking about me to Miss Webb. And I didn't care who else they told. Or what they told them.

When Tory-boy finally came out, he really wanted to go see someone. Some girl, I guess.

"Esau, I swear I won't be but an hour. That's if I go now. But if I have to drive you back home first—"

"You think Miss Dyson is going to want me sitting out here for an hour, Tory-boy?"

"No. No, Esau. I didn't even ask her. I mean, she knew where I was going, and she asked if you wouldn't like to take some tea with her. I said I'd ask you. So I am."

I was about to tell Tory-boy I'd have to check for myself when Miss Jayne Dyson came to the screen door.

"That is exactly what I asked Tory," she said, like she was reading my thoughts. "I could use some company. That's why I always like seeing Tory. He's a real gentleman, and I know who taught him that."

"I . . ." That was as far as I got—I guess I ran out of words. Miss Dyson held the screen door open, and Tory-boy wheeled me right inside. I swear our van was moving before Miss Dyson even got a chance to sit herself down.

I n the fall, darkness drops down quick. But I couldn't really tell what time it was by the light—Miss Dyson had her parlor fixed so that it was always in some kind of soft shadow.

I probably pay more attention to couches and chairs and such because I don't know what it would be like to sit in them. Hers were old-style: built of a heavy, dark wood; the cushions covered with a kind of a velvety material as dark as dried blood.

Every other time I'd been there, Miss Dyson would always seat herself on the divan, so there could be a long, low table between us. For putting cups and saucers on without making it awkward for me. But this time, she put herself in a high-backed straight chair near the corner. When she beckoned with her hand, I rolled my chair over to her. Fussing a little to myself about the wheels making marks on her carpet, but I could see she wasn't paying attention. Or didn't care about such things.

"You just wait here a minute," she told me.

I don't know how long she was gone. I was—I don't know how to say it, exactly—maybe *feeling* the parlor. My eyes closed, and I was breathing through my nose. . . .

"You take honey?"

I had to come back from wherever I'd gone to, and I wasn't sure I heard her last word right, so I just nodded.

"Lemon?"

"Yes, I do," I answered, feeling better now that I was back all the way.

"Not sugar, though?"

"With that honey? No, ma'am."

"I thought I told you—"

"I didn't mean it like it came out," I told her. "I was just trying to be . . . emphatic."

"Clear."

"Clear," I agreed.

We sipped our tea, polite as a church social. Then she put her cup and saucer down on the little table and leaned toward me, dropping her voice just a little. Miss Dyson never spoke loudly, but this was . . . not so much quieter as it was softer.

"I know what you do, Esau," she half-whispered. It didn't feel like an accusation. More like it was something I should be proud of.

I wouldn't disrespect her by making a joke. And I couldn't well deny what hadn't been said. So I just put down my own cup and saucer and folded my hands, like I was expecting her to go on.

"I don't judge you for it," she said. "I've been judged, and I know how that kind of meanness feels when you're on the receiving end of it."

"Miss Dyson, I would never—"

"Lord, did you think I was talking about you when I said that, Esau?"

"Well . . . no, I suppose you wouldn't do that. But I just wanted to make certain you knew—"

"Esau Till, you can stop all that. Right this minute. It was me telling you, not the other way around."

I wasn't sure what she meant. Not exactly. So I was grateful when she broke the silence. "Does cigarette smoke bother you?"

"Not at all," I lied, but it felt right to do it then.

She jumped up and ran off. Back almost before I knew it. But she wasn't in her chair; she was on her knees, next to me.

"It's easier this way," she said, handing me a lighter.

I knew what to do with that—just part of good manners. I fired up the lighter, and held the flame until she got her cigarette going. Then I watched as she put the ashtray on the table with the cups and saucers.

I couldn't help looking down her dress when she did that. When I realized what that would make me look like, I straightened up quick.

She took a short little puff on her cigarette. Ladylike, I guess it was. Then she said, "I was close to twelve. I remember because my twelfth birthday was coming, and I was hoping for . . . Well, it doesn't matter. That's how old I was when a terrible thing happened to me."

"What was—?"

"It doesn't matter," she shushed me. "Not anymore, it doesn't. By the ninth grade, people were talking about me. Behind their hands, but I could see it in their eyes. And the boys, they made it impossible for me to stay here."

"You went away?"

"For a time I did, yes. But I came back. Maybe ten years later it was, but it might as well have been the day I left. Only, by then, I knew how to turn their meanness into money."

I didn't say anything. Just watched her puff on her cigarette a couple more times.

"Some of us, we get marked," Miss Dyson said. "Me, not even twelve. And you, from the moment you were born. But those kind of marks aren't any stupid 666 brand, like some wish they were. What they really are is trail markers. And we, all of us with those kind of marks, we're bound to follow them."

"You didn't have to come home."

"Home?" She kind of laughed. "No, Esau. I didn't have to come back here. Any more than you didn't have to stay."

I opened my mouth to tell her about Tory-boy, but then I snapped it shut when it came to me that she knew all about that. Wasn't I the one who'd brought him to her in the first place?

"Are you familiar with what they call the Bernoulli effect?" I asked her instead.

"No. No, I surely never heard of anything like that. Why do you ask?"

"If you force smoke through a pipe, the more narrow the pipe, the faster the smoke will move. Think of it as if you blew your cigarette smoke through a soda straw."

"Ah! So, if you only have one road to go down, a real narrow one . . ."

"You'll move faster than the others. Be ahead of the field by the first lap. That's a scientific truth. And that's how I always saw you, myself."

"There's nothing wrong with you, Esau. Not one damn thing."

I didn't know what to say. I didn't see how she could say such things to a man in a wheelchair.

"If you'll trust me, I can give you something," she said, so soft I could feel the words brush against my cheek. "I can give you something you thought you could never have."

"What could you—?"

"Do you trust me, Esau?"

Her eyes only left me but one answer. "Yes" is all I said.

Before Tory-boy came back, Miss Dyson had healed me. I don't mean like a doctor. Or a preacher, either. Only a person marked like we both were could ever really do what she'd done, and then only for another of our own kind.

For the first time, I was glad I wasn't really paralyzed below the waist. I would have traded every pain I'd ever felt in my whole life for what Miss Dyson showed me I could do.

When she was done—when I was done, I guess I mean—she just stood up and walked off.

She came back quick enough. All she'd done was put some retouching on her face.

Something, something powerful, told me that if I had offered her money then, I would have lost something more than precious. Something I could never replace.

When she said, "Now, you have to promise to do something for me," I thought maybe she wanted somebody to die. But I didn't really know her, not then.

"Now—and from this moment on—you have to call me by my name," she said. "Jayne. That's my name, Esau. Jayne."

went to see her any number of times after that. Tory-boy would drive me over, and come back whenever I told him to. Once I got him a cell phone, I didn't even have to say a word. One ring followed by a hang-up, Tory-boy would know it was me.

At first, there wasn't but one way we could . . . make love. I feel I have a right to call it that, because I know what was in my own heart. I had to lie on my back, and Jayne would kind of straddle me.

Later, she showed me some other things. They all worked, too. I mean, I worked. No, that's wrong. Nothing we ever did was work. What I'm trying to say is that parts of me worked.

It was as if everything had come full circle. I remembered how proud Tory-boy had been when he was telling me he could cast spells himself. How he could turn a girl into a lady, by treating her like one. But that spell only worked if she believed she was a lady herself.

I realized, lying there, my arms around Jayne as I kept myself inside her, that she must have believed what she told me, too, that first time. She wasn't casting any spell; she knew.

I must've gotten lost in that thought, because the next thing I remember was, Jayne started panting like she'd just run a race, making little gasping sounds. She bucked so hard I was afraid she'd come loose from me, but she put her face down and bit into the pillow I'd learned to slip under my head.

I don't know how to write down the sound she made before she collapsed against my chest. But she recovered quick enough.

"Don't stop, Esau. You're not done yet. Come on!"

You want to know what that was all about, don't you?" she said, a few minutes later.

"Not if you—"

"Ssssh. That was an orgasm, Esau. That's what you have every time when you . . . shoot off inside me. It's not the same for a woman. We don't feel such things in only one place; it takes over our whole bodies."

"But you never—"

"Did that before? Of course not. I didn't even know I could. Listen to me go on. I know what they're supposed to feel like—I've faked them often enough."

"Why would you do that?"

"Not every man wants the same thing, Esau. Most of them, all they care about is satisfying themselves. But there's always a few that want to believe they're such bulls in the bedroom that they can make any woman . . . come, that's the word they use. Any woman, even a whore."

"You're no—"

She put two fingers over my lips. "Not to you, Esau. I know that. Just like you're no . . . client to me. I knew you were a very special kind of man the first time I ever met you."

"I—"

"Shush, now. I'm telling you things of value. It's kind of a tradition around here for men to bring their sons to a . . . to an experienced woman for their first time. But they don't really want their boys to learn anything, not from a woman like me. The only lesson they want taught is that there are women so low you can pay them to have sex with you.

"But you, you wanted Tory-boy to learn to be gentle. To kiss a girl sweet. None of these men wanted their boys to kiss a . . . woman like me at all. They didn't want them to learn how to talk, how to caress, how to . . . well, really, how to do anything at all. What they wanted is to be able to take their boys down to wherever they hang out and brag that he's a man now."

"So, when a boy like that gets full-grown, when he gets married, what does he know about . . . doing it right?" I asked her.

"*Nothing* is what he knows. Why do you think they're all brought up to marry virgins? How is someone going to spot your ignorance if they're ignorant themselves?"

"That all seems so . . . Well, you said it yourself just now: ignorant."

"That doesn't matter. Not to the men. If their wives don't know what to do, there's always women like me."

"But there are folks who love each other. I know there are."

"Don't confuse those things, Esau. Just because a man may be faithful, he'll still feel it's up to the woman to make him happy. And the only way a man is going to be happy is if he thinks he's got the magic touch when it comes to his own woman."

"How would he know that?"

"Remember what I said before? About faking an orgasm? Well, for that, a woman has to be good. Good and kind, both. Faking the orgasm, that's just a skill. Something you can learn; something you can get good at doing. With most men, you don't even have to be all that good to fool them, because they *want* to be fooled.

"But kindness, that isn't faking it at all. There's nothing in that for the woman, you might think. But you'd be wrong. Doing a kindness because you want to make your man feel more like a man, that's love. True love."

"So, before, you—"

"Just stop right now! You're supposed to be such a genius, can't you use your mind? If I was faking—before, I mean—if I was faking just to be kind, why in the world would I explain how that works? In this bed, that first time, the only virgin there was you. Understand? That was you, trusting me. Can't you keep on doing that, Esau?"

"I never stopped," I told her. And it was the truth.

Maybe Lansdale had just used me to get rid of an old enemy, the way Judakowski had sent that hyped-up young man into Lansdale's bar a year or so back.

Or maybe he was showing me real respect by knowing I'd want to square accounts with Judakowski my own self. The way a man should.

None of that matters. If it wasn't for Jayne being gone, I never would have told a word of how she'd healed me.

But I don't mind admitting that when she'd said "honey" that night, it made me think of the first woman to ever use that word on me.

I don't even mind admitting that I couldn't wait to drop in at Lansdale's bar. Once I'd made sure it was a night Nancy would be working, that is.

Maybe it's just as well my hand was forced. Sooner or later, the day would have come when Tory-boy wouldn't have been able to drive me home. So what difference was there between the hospital and the penitentiary?

Even after Judakowski, I wasn't in any danger. Nobody was going to suspect me of such a thing. Yes, Judakowski always had a lot of jobs out. What happened to him can certainly happen when a man doesn't get paid for work he did. But even the cops who knew what I did and who I did it for, they believed I only worked long-distance. How else is a cripple going to shoot anyone, especially a wary man like Judakowski had been?

Judakowski was right to be wary. I doubt there was a person in the world he could truly trust. His men weren't with him the way Lansdale's men were with him. They were nothing but a paid labor force, and they had to know that.

You can buy obedience, but you can't buy the kind of loyalty that makes a man throw himself between a pistol and his boss.

Lansdale might have had plenty of worries—being shot in the back was never one of them.

Everything had been going along just perfect until those master-race morons showed Tory-boy a club he could join. Not some club that maybe might let him in if he did things for them; this club, they wanted him for himself.

"I'm a pure Aryan, Esau!" he told me, all excited. "See, there's ice people and mud people, and I got the perfect blood in me. They're a great group of guys. And they understand, too. The first night, they tried to get me to have beers with them. I told them I can't do that. Mostly, when I say that, folks look at me funny. But not them, Esau. After I told them I had to keep bad stuff out of my body, they looked at me like I was just talking sense.

"The leader, he even said I was the ideal example! Pure, clean living, that was the way to build our race."

I thought it would pass. Tory-boy could get all excited about something and then forget about it by the next day.

But it only got worse. One morning at breakfast, Tory-boy told me he had a new girlfriend. "They picked her for me, Esau. And guess why! 'Cause we've got the best blood. She's pure white, too. So we're going to make babies. We're going to uplift our race!"

I knew that was never going to happen. Years ago, I'd had Tory-boy fixed. I got the doctor to read the medical records, and he agreed a vasectomy would be "in the young man's best interests." With me signing as guardian, it was all over in an hour.

Tory-boy didn't know why he was getting the "operation." When I told him it had to be done, otherwise he could end up in a wheelchair like me, that was all it took.

I needn't have bothered with all that. Tory-boy knew I never would do anything that wasn't good for him, no matter what.

It would be a while before those skinhead imbeciles found out Tory-boy couldn't make babies, but they already knew what he could do with a baseball bat.

They didn't need Tory-boy, but they sure knew how to use him. When he told me about going out on "actions" with his "brothers," I knew it was just a matter of time before they killed someone. And who would end up taking the blame for it.

I couldn't put protection on Tory-boy anymore. He had learned too much new stuff. He wasn't exactly sure why muds and homos and race traitors were all controlled by the Jews, much less why they all had to be exterminated. Still, he was ready to do his part.

I guess he didn't remember the real reason why the Beast had killed Rory-Anne that long-ago night. Telling him nigger cock was much better than his was the same as her *asking* him to do it.

I felt my heart start to crack in my chest, stress fractures already forming on its surface.

had almost waited too long. When Tory-boy came home and showed me the swastika tattooed on his arm, that's when I knew things had changed forever.

Not because of the tattoo—because he hadn't asked me first.

That's when Tory-boy told me he needed the tattoo because a real important meeting was due to happen the very next month. The big leader himself was coming all the way from Louisville to speak. Men were driving from Columbus, Cincinnati, Pittsburgh, Wheeling, Richmond . . . and a lot of other places. He couldn't be the only one there without what he called "White Power ink," could he?

The night of that important meeting, I suffered some kind of attack. It was so bad I could hardly speak, and my upper body was locked up so tight I couldn't get much of a breath, either.

Tory-boy picked me up, carried me to the van, and drove me to the emergency room, paying no attention to red lights or stop signs.

When they took me in the back, the doctors told him he couldn't stay there with me. Tory-boy didn't move. So some young doctor called for the security guards. But they were local boys, and they told the doctor they weren't about to get themselves broken into pieces over nothing—all the young man wanted to do was stay with his brother, what was so wrong about that?

That really infuriated the doctor. He ordered a nurse to call the police. She told him, "I'm sorry, sir, but you're not from around here. Trust me, the police won't come, not if you tell them who it is you want them to try and haul out."

It took a long time to run all their tests. They had my whole medical history there, and they could see I'd never had a seizure before. The doctors were puzzled, but doctors never admit that, so they kept at it for a long time before they said I was "stabilized," but I'd have to go over to the state hospital for more tests pretty soon.

Tory-boy probably thought his "brothers" would understand, once he explained why he'd missed the big meeting.

Maybe someday he'll find another club that will want him to join.

The one he used to be in is gone, and I don't think there'll be another one taking its place, not around here. I can't see them trying to start up a new operation in the same town where seventy-nine of them were all inside a concrete building—Tory-boy said they called it "The Bunker"—when a series of sequential explosions turned the whole thing into a giant incinerator.

Every one of them cremated, like they told Tory-boy they were going to do to the Jews someday.

The very next day—a Wednesday, it was—Tory-boy and I went for a long ride, all the way to the state capital. The people I make things for told me where I could find a needle artist who'd know better than to remember things. His shop was always closed on Wednesdays anyway.

That man knew his work. He turned Tory-boy's swastika into a big butterfly. A black butterfly, outlined in red, with just a touch of gold beneath.

Tory-boy never flinched all the time the needle was working on him. He never feels pain in his body.

All his pain is in his blood.

So now you know. You know the only crime I ever got caught clean for was by accident. I don't mean I didn't intend it; I just mean I never imagined the kind of investigation it would launch. How could I know the FBI had an informant planted in with those Nazi people? That's how they knew every single person who was supposed to be in that cement tomb. And that's how they knew who *wasn't* there when their man got blown to bits.

And they only knew that much because plenty of folks had seen Tory-boy around after the concrete oven had done its job—there were no bodies inside that anyone could hope to identify.

So, when they came out to the house after that, they came in force. The only way to save the dogs was to tell Tory-boy to let them pass. Otherwise, the men wearing all that body armor would have had their chance to use those machine guns and other toys they couldn't wait to play with. Tory-boy would have tried to stop them, and their gunning down his dogs would've turned him into a monster worse than anything those men had ever imagined.

Once they got inside the house, they surprised me by acting so polite. But I was a match for them in that department. I knew Tory-boy would be anxious, what with all those people and cars around, but I never let it show.

They told me what they already knew, and I didn't blink. But once they showed me their own agent's field reports, once I did the math and worked out the dates, I saw there wasn't but one way to save Tory-boy.

I knew that the Feds had their own courts, but that didn't concern me. Once we had the deal worked out, I knew I wouldn't be gone more than a week or two before being sent back home. That's how long it would take for me to plead guilty.

I had to make sure I took that plea in front of people who didn't know me. The way the law works is, you can plead guilty all you want, but it's a jury gets to set the penalty.

I couldn't be sure that local folks would look all that unfavorably on me killing all those Nazis. It wasn't like you could find a lot of liberals around here, but I couldn't imagine any of them shaving their heads, or wearing those silly costumes. Those Nazis might be all white, but they were still all strangers.

But of all the things that separated us, I think it's music that would create the widest chasm. Around here, people *respect* music. I don't mean "today's hits" or that video garbage—once you're in our hearts, we never forget you. So, even if WWVA isn't the king of radio anymore, Hank Williams is never going to give up his throne.

Lansdale never said, and I never asked, but I felt I knew why he named his little nightingale "Patsy," too.

All those White Power people did with *their* music was make a lot of noise. It wasn't just that nobody from around here bought their CDs; nobody from around here would want anyone to think their music was *our* music.

So my own people might not want to sentence me to death, but outsiders didn't speak our language, and I knew that confessing to all the *other* murders I'd committed would guarantee I'd get what I wanted.

I hadn't known the Feds had a plant in with those Nazis, but it didn't matter. I knew the truth, deep inside myself. I was—I don't know any other word for it—jealous. I should have been satisfied that, no matter what, I'd never lose Tory-boy's love. I should have been pleased that he'd shown he was a lot smarter than I'd given him credit for. I knew that because he didn't tell me about those skinheads until he'd *already* joined up; Tory-boy had known exactly what I would have said if he'd asked me first.

And that tattoo.

I would have killed them all for that alone. Killed them because I wanted them dead.

If I could have turned my hate into explosives, there wouldn't be any of them left, anywhere.

That's how I ended up here, telling my true story. I don't know when anyone will read it—it could be pretty soon; it could be decades.

If it turns out that I'm never betrayed, the final timing is all up to Miss Webb. I'd taught Tory-boy to mind her just like he did me. We were holding hands, Miss Webb and me, when I told him that for the first time.

And if Miss Webb—if Evangeline—was my . . . my woman, that was enough. Tory-boy always minded his big brother, so it made perfect sense to him that he had to mind his sister-in-law. He might not know about legalities, but my Tory-boy knew me. And he knew I'd made my choice.

T here were some complications involved in order for them all to get together and give me the assurances I needed. But they managed it.

When everyone turned their cards faceup, the hands looked like this: the State could clear dozens of unsolved killings on their books with the statements I was going to make when I pleaded guilty, but it would be a federal jury that would pronounce the sentence.

The deal was fair all around. The Feds wanted some things. The local DA had his own list. And there was something I wanted, too. It would take years for them to execute me, and I had to be near Tory-boy—as near as I could get—until it happened.

When everybody knew their role, the Feds read me a list of agents who'd been murdered within my reach. I picked a bomb that had been planted in the car of an FBI agent who worked way north of here.

In fact, that's where they started. They had this big map loaded onto the computer, so it could project on a huge screen. Our house was in the center of that map, and they had different-colored circles around it.

Concentric circles, like when you throw a rock into a pond. Whenever they moved the circles away from our house, the readout in miles would show in a corner of the screen.

The map was dotted with black "X" marks. One for every murdered agent whose killer had never been found.

When they first activated the screen, sure enough, a black "X" popped up where that Nazi bunker had been.

I hadn't known I was signing my own confession when I blew up that bunker. But it wouldn't have stopped me if I had.

What did shock me a little was seeing another black "X" where that motorcycle gang had set up their hangar so many years ago.

I guess about the only place the Feds didn't have their hooks in around where I lived was with the local bosses. Or maybe they did; if they were still alive and undercover, they wouldn't have shown up on the map.

That's how I ended up here. Coming home while I waited to die was my choice, and I was intractable on that score.

I couldn't risk waiting for the needle anyplace other than close to home. I had to make sure they kept me in a place where Tory-boy could visit.

I had to be in a place where I could still get messages out when I needed to. A place where I could still do business.

And maybe, if the prison was as open to cash-money deals as the men who've been here say, maybe even a chance to kiss my Evangeline goodbye.

I will keep my end of the bargain. Lansdale and Judakowski, they're both gone now. That doesn't change a thing.

Judakowski was one killing I'd never confessed to. It happened just before they caught me, but I'd still had a number of opportunities to meet with the new boss of his gang.

"Lou Money" was what he went by—I didn't know if that was his real name, and it didn't matter to me. Didn't matter to me that some even say he was the one who'd put Judakowski on the spot. Lou Money knows better himself. I made sure he knew. I told him every detail, and I knew he had his own sources inside the local cops, so he could find out for himself that I'd told him the truth.

That was very important to me, that Lou Money knew I told the truth. That was because I told him the truth of how Judakowski had been killed, but I lied about the reason. What I told Lou Money was that Judakowski had broken his word to me, and Tory-boy almost got himself in deep trouble as a result. I couldn't have something like that *ever* happen.

Lou Money was a very understanding man. He'd make a good boss.

So Judakowski's gone. And Lansdale's not around anymore, either. He died in a fire. The way I heard it, he was doing some business with a man who lived in a trailer, way outside of town. They were still talking out in the yard when the trailer just blazed up. Everyone started running away. Then one of the trailer's windows broke out and they could hear a woman screaming inside.

That stopped them dead in their tracks—the man they were doing business with, he was supposed to be living there alone. The woman was wrapped in flames, but they could still hear her screaming. When Lansdale heard "My baby!" he just spun around, wrapped his coat over his head, and charged into the trailer before any of his men could stop him.

It must have seemed like forever, but Lansdale finally burst out of the trailer, bringing some of the fire with him.

His men had been standing there with their own coats off, ready to beat out the flames. But they could see they were too late. The way it's told, nothing was left of Lansdale but a burned-to-the-bone thing of disfigured horror.

There'd be no open-casket funeral for Lansdale, but the baby he went after was alive. The baby had some burned flesh, but they got him to the hospital in time to save him.

I heard they shipped him off to the Shriners, and he's going to be as good as new, eventually. Folks say the Lord was watching over that baby. If that's true, I guess Lansdale went out doing the Lord's work. That's about as squared-up as a man can get.

How do I know all this? It's not complicated. Lansdale wasn't like Judakowski. Not only didn't he think he could never be replaced, he had named his own successor a long time ago, and he made sure everyone knew it. Including me.

Coy came to see me on a visit. His name wasn't on the list every Death Row inmate is supposed to file with the Warden's office, but they never enforced any of those rules any too strictly with me.

Coy was still too young to carry himself like Lansdale, but I could see he was following clear footsteps, and he'd walk to the end of that road. Coming to visit me, that was sending a message. And taking a risk to do it. But I knew Lansdale would have expected nothing less.

All I really knew about Coy—he must have written down his last name to get inside for the visit, but he never told it to me—was that he was some kind of martial-arts expert. And the story people tell about that does sound embellished a bit.

The story was this: Lansdale was holding a sit-down at the bar he owned, The Blues ByYou. It pulls in a pretty rough crowd, but everybody knows you leave your attitude at the door.

Regulars knew the signals. Like if Chester Phillips took off the black pullover he always wore. Chester could sweep a few balls off the pool table into that pullover and grab both ends in one hand before you could blink. He had this spinning motion he'd do, which always ended with that loaded pullover striking someone. Whatever Chester hit with that move was going to break, and his preference was for heads.

Maybe the young man who walked in the door that night was looking to make a name for himself. Nobody had ever seen him before, but he must have known something about how things work. He walked right past Chester and over to Lansdale's table.

It was Coy he wanted. He cursed him out every way you could imagine, going way over the line that people call "fighting words."

Coy just ignored him. As long as the stranger didn't put his hands on anyone, nobody was going to so much as acknowledge his presence.

All his challenge-talk finally got out of hand—he was making so much noise that Lansdale had to tell the young man to leave.

"You gonna throw me out, old man?" He must have been well past crazy to say something like that. Or his veins were running wild with meth courage. Maybe even both.

That's when Coy stood up from the table. He wasn't a bouncer or anything, but the other man had singled him out first, so he was the natural choice.

No sooner did Coy stand up than the hyped-up guy whipped out a push-button stiletto and snapped the blade to life.

Eugene folded his hands on top of the table. That should have told the young man something right there—you flash a knife in front of Eugene, you're going to end up contributing to a blood bank the Red Cross never heard of. But Eugene was a surgeon, not a coroner. Folding his hands like he did, that was the same as telling the other man he was already as good as done.

The young man didn't know Eugene, so he couldn't read the smoke signal.

"Son," Lansdale called over to him, "didn't your daddy ever tell you not to bring a knife to a gunfight?"

The young man watched as Coy walked toward him, both hands held in front of him, palms up, like he was waiting for something to fall.

"I don't see no gun," the young man said as he slashed the air in front of him. He handled the knife like a man having an epileptic fit.

Coy just kept closing the distance, moving slow, like he was worried about that blade. The only person in the whole bar who might have believed that was the demented fool flashing it.

While he was still too far away for a knife to reach him, Coy shot out his left foot. There was a sound like plastic bubble-wrap popping and crackling at the same time. You didn't need a medical license to know the knife-man's kneecap was shattered.

Coy sure didn't. He'd already turned around and was walking back to the table before the guy with the blade hit the floor.

The young man was shrieking like a bat using its sonar to hunt in the dark. The only word you could make out was "Hospital!"

Nobody in the bar looked his way. At the back table, everybody stayed quiet, waiting for Lansdale to speak.

"That better be a cell phone you're reaching for," Lansdale told the young man. "Use it to call a cab. And be sure to tell them you'll be waiting on the sidewalk. Outside."

One of the waitresses opened the door, then slid a chair in place to keep it open. Somehow, the guy dragged himself outside.

Lansdale really died a hero, saving that baby like he did," I told Coy that day he visited.

"Yeah, he did. Good thing we'd come in two cars. If we'd had to wait until Eugene was finished carving up that scumbag, the baby might not have made it."

"Why would Eugene—?"

"Could've been because that miserable little piece of shit had told us he lived in that trailer alone. Could've been because he was such a foul weasel that he just walked away when that fire broke out—that had to be his woman who broke out the window, probably his baby, too.

"Could even have been that Eugene figured that slimeball was responsible for Mr. Lansdale's death. Me, I never asked him."

truly believed both Lou Money and Coy would keep the word their bosses had given me all those years ago. For different reasons, sure: Lansdale wasn't a boss to Coy; he was family, and that means certain things would be expected of him. Whatever anyone expected of Lou Money didn't matter—he wasn't going to risk his whole operation being exposed over the little bit of it I was asking him to keep secret.

The reasons didn't matter—both men's word would stay as rock-hard as the men whose positions they had inherited.

I'm still relying on that, but I can't see into the future.

That wasn't enough protection to satisfy me. Giving one man power isn't a guarantee he'll use it right.

So, if Tory-boy ever got a call from the one person I told him he could always trust, my little brother would go down to our mine. Then he'd finish it just the way I'd taught him. All he'd have to do was push a button.

That same person who I told Tory-boy he could always trust would mail out one final package. That one would have everything I had on each of the two operations.

I didn't know what Lansdale's son would do with that pile of information, but I had a pretty good idea.

'd set all that up way before I was handed another card to play. For this town, a trump ace.

No matter how I phrase this, it still comes down to trust. That's a very complicated thing, trust. I'd felt obligated to kill Jackhammer Judakowski for what he'd done to Miss Jayne Dyson. And a big part of that obligation was that she had trusted me to do it.

Not in so many words, maybe. Even with the life she had to live, how could she have expected it to end as ugly as it did? No, the trust obligation came when she handed me a stick of dynamite late one night.

"I was going to be a secretary, Esau. Imagine that. Ah, it doesn't matter, not now. See this? I bought this steno pad before I even enrolled in school. And I never wrote a single word in it. But I did bring it with me when I decided to come home, and now it's about full up.

"It's not one of those 'little black books,' but it holds the same information you'd expect to find in one, understand?"

"Why are you giving this to me, Jayne?"

"I'm not giving it to you, Esau. I'm asking you to hold it for me. Hold it in a safe place, a place only you know about.

"If you go first, I won't need it. And, most likely, you won't need it if I go before you. But if anything should happen to me—something bad, I mean; something deliberately done—the name of the man who caused it to happen will be in my steno pad. You'll know what to do with it then, won't you?"

"Yes" is all I said. But I knew I was taking on a debt with that one word. And I wasn't lying when I told her, "I'd be proud, Jayne."

So I've got even more than the records I kept on myself and my work. Judakowski is already finished; in fact, he was gone before I ever looked in Jayne's steno pad. And now that steno pad was a weapon all by itself. It might not put anyone in jail, or get them killed, but it would sure teach certain people the high price of hypocrisy.

Like I said: trust. Who else but Miss Webb would I have left any of this with?

But I wouldn't have been able to sleep a single night if I hadn't allowed for possibilities beyond the knowledge of any mortal man. So, if Miss Webb doesn't show up in person to claim all three of her copies by a certain date, well, there's two more copies. And those just go out by themselves.

If she goes where I told her to go, she'll not only find the books, she'll find a laptop computer, too. All she'd have to do is plug it in and turn it on. A screen would come up, with only two choices: SEND or DO *NOT* SEND.

Miss Webb knows, should she press that SEND link, my story, my *true* story, will be all over the world in minutes. I told her a long while back that I couldn't tell the total truth without her name coming out—I cautioned her about that, more than once.

But she never wavered. That was the way she wanted it, too, she told me.

"I'll make sure of it, Esau. I swear on my heart. I'll make sure of every single thing, even if I have to go down in your mine with Tory-boy and hold his hand while he presses that button."

That's the wonder of knowing the date of your own death in advance. I could leave in peace, because I had protected my baby brother all the way up to the time when he'd join me.

And I had people watching. People who knew they had to wait six months to hear from Miss Webb. If they didn't get a DO *NOT* SEND message by then, they were going to launch my last bomb.

Over the years, I had gotten to be friends with two different Internet investigators. One's out in the Mojave somewhere, the other's in Norway. They both might be a little off-center, but they wouldn't have to do any more with what I'd be putting in their hands than Tory-boy would if he ended up down in our mine.

Just push a button, and wait for the explosion.

I don't want to be associated with the other men in this place, not even in the minds of whoever might be reading this.

Yes, there's some here that the State shouldn't be killing. Why kill a man who heard voices inside his head commanding him, voices he couldn't disobey? Why kill a man whose IQ is so low that he doesn't even know where he is, or what's waiting on him?

I feel sympathy for those men, but no kinship with them. I knew what I was doing when I did it, and the result was the one I'd intended.

So, if anyone's reading this, they know there was more than enough good reasons for the State to take my life.

Some are here—on Death Row, I mean—only because they had lousy lawyers. One guy, he and his partner robbed a store. They took one of the clerks with them, to make sure nobody called the police until they set her free. Only that never happened.

The partner got a life sentence in exchange for telling the police where the girl's body was hidden. The other one, the one that's going to be executed, he didn't get the same deal. Which is double-wrong, because the guy who got the break was the one who raped that girl before he shot her in the head. At least that's what the man here says.

I do agree that what happened in that case was unfair. But I don't think it should be fixed by giving the condemned man a life sentence. No, what I think is that his partner should be right here with him.

The mystical word on Death Row is "DNA." There must be over a dozen men here who claim to be purely innocent. All it would take to set them free is this magic test.

I wonder if they actually believe that.

It was Miss Jayne Dyson who showed me that I wasn't really dead below my waist. But it was Miss Webb who showed me that my heart wasn't closed to everyone but Tory-boy, as I'd always believed.

That's why, if you're reading this, you get to hear me say what only one other living soul has ever heard.

I love you, Evangeline.

The guards have promised they'll let me wheel myself into the Execution Chamber. We shook hands on that, and I believe they will keep their word.

I've come to think highly of some of them, and I think they regard me the same way. Not all of them, of course. The ones who tried to get me to give them something they could sell, they finally gave up. "No hard feelings," they assured me. But even if they were telling the truth, they were only talking about their own feelings.

I've been rotting long enough. I don't need any more stays of execution. I only waited this long until I could be sure my last bomb was built, and that the detonator was in the right hands.

I've only got a little time left to me, no matter where I spend it.

This is where it ends. Me and this story, both.

I apologize to nobody on this earth. This is no plea for forgiveness. I know I don't deserve forgiveness, and I'm not looking for any. I did the best I was capable of, and your judgments have no more meaning for me now than they ever did.

But there will be judgments; I'm convinced of that. I think

about all the different people I've run across in my life. I think about them all the time. And what I think is that almost all of them should stop pointing their fingers and get themselves down to church. Fall down on their knees and pray.

Pray there is no God.

don't know where I'm going after they wheel the gurney away with my lifeless body strapped to it. But one thing I know for sure. If there's another place beyond this one, I'll get there under my own power.

Don't doubt me.

My name is Esau Till.

New from hard-boiled
crime fiction master

Andrew Vachss

"A handful are as good.
None are better." —*People*

Aftershock

An idyllic seacoast village hides
a horrifying rite of passage....

HC ISBN: 978-0-307-90774-5
EBK ISBN: 978-0-307-90775-2

Coming in June 2013
from Pantheon Books